MARILYN SINGER

Hyperion Books for Children
NEW YORK

Thanks to Kathleen Cotter, Donn Livingston,
Asher Williams, and to Andrea Cascardi
and everyone else at Hyperion Books for Children

Text © 1993 by Marilyn Singer.
All rights reserved. Printed in the United States of America.
For more information address Hyperion Books for Children,
114 Fifth Avenue, New York, New York 10011.

First Edition
1 3 5 7 9 10 8 6 4 2

Library of Congress Catalog Card Number: 93-31912
ISBN: 1-56282-583-6

To Steve, of course

—M. S.

CHAPTER

ONE

I t's hard to hold your nose and steer your bike at the same time. Especially when you're riding down a dark, bumpy road on a moonless night with a heavy load of very old, very dead fish you're about to dump in somebody's swimming pool.

It wasn't hard getting the fish. Just a quick visit to the Dumpster out back of Sharkey's Market with a cardboard box, and I had all I could carry. It wasn't hard sneaking out of my house either to do the deed. Mom and Dad both sleep like a pair of chipmunks in winter. So you could say things might've been a whole lot worse.

On the other hand, you could say things might be a whole lot better if I had my buddy Tag along to help out. Or Mike and Corey or the rest of my gang. But if they were here, I wouldn't be doing this in the first place, now would I?

You can't see my destination from the road,

which is good because nobody there can see me either. It's a big old house, and a fancy one, too, set back among the trees and bushes, with gates and columns and a long, sweeping driveway. Just a few weeks ago the gates were rusty, the columns cracked, and the driveway was covered with weeds up to my knees. Now everything's been plastered and painted and the driveway's covered with gravel. White gravel that gleams in my little headlight. It's very inviting, that gravel-covered driveway. It makes you want to follow it right up to the house the way old Dorothy trotted on up her yellow brick road to Oz.

But I know better than to do that. Instead I zip past the driveway to the big beech tree carved with everybody's initials. My headlight picks out a brand-new pair of them: "B. O. and P. U. Forever." Somebody ought to get himself a new name, a new girlfriend, or both, I snicker to myself—but softly, because sound travels funny out here, and I don't want anybody to hear me laughing.

Just beyond the tree is a little turnoff that leads through a gap in a fence to a shortcut straight to the pool. That's where I ditch my bike. I'm praying nobody's fixed that gap yet or I'm sunk. I hoist the box off the bike and start walking. If I thought the fish were heavy and smelly before, there's no way to describe just how much they weigh and stink now that I'm carrying them on my shoulder. But, hey, there's no use complaining, and nobody to complain to.

2

When I reach the fence, I find that I'm in luck. The gap's still there, and it's maybe even a little wider. I squeeze through with the carton and start down the shortcut. It's even darker here than on the road, and now I don't even have my headlight. A branch pokes me in the ear. Mosquitoes buzz around my face and hands, biting me anywhere they feel like it. A briar whips across my ankles and sticks to my sock. I hear a faint rip as I walk on, pulling it free.

It's not a real steamy night, but I'm sweating pretty good anyway. I can hear myself breathing kind of hard, too, along with a lot of other sounds. You'd think it would be quiet out here now, but it's noisy as a school cafeteria at lunchtime, what with the crickets and the katydids and who knows what else carrying on. To my right, a bullfrog burps in a bubbling little stream. To my left, something fast and probably furry skitters into the bushes. I hope its name isn't Little Flower and that, if it is, it's got better things to do than squirt me with its perfume.

And I keep on walking.

At the end of the path, I know there's a low stone wall. I also know I won't be able to see it or feel it with my hands, which are occupied. When I figure I've nearly reached it, I go slow as a baby taking its first steps, to make sure I don't bump into it and mess up my knees. When my big toe stubs rock, I know I'm there.

Carefully, I set down the box on the wall and hop over. I take a few seconds to wipe the sweat off my face and scratch all my bug bites, which are starting to itch something fierce. Then I lift up the carton once more. Only half a football field to go and I'm there, I tell myself, squeezing through a row of hedges onto neatly trimmed grass.

Soon, I see it. The pool. Black as a tar pit under the stars. Way off is the house, and it's dark, too, just the way I hoped it would be. I stare toward the windows. I can't see them, but I take a guess at which one's his. "Good night. Sleep nice and tight. Don't wake up till the morning light, turkey," I rasp. I stride forward, and my leg sinks into a hole up to my calf. The box goes flying, and I fall flat on my face.

For one minute, all I can do is lie there, stunned. For the next minute, I'm still lying there, staring at the house to see if any lights go on, if anyone heard the noise. But they don't, and they didn't.

Finally, I manage to sit up and check all my body parts. Nothing's busted, but my left knee's burning with what feels like a nasty scrape. I flex it. Yeah, it's a big bruise all right. My leg's gonna be good and stiff soon, so I've got to finish up—and fast.

I grope around, expecting to find fish all over the lawn. But amazingly, the box is intact, still taped shut. I take it over to the pool, tear off the tape, and slide the fish into the water, so nice and easy they barely make a splash.

When I'm done, I stand up and look at the still, dark house once more. "Sunrise. Open your eyes. You're gonna get a big surprise," I rhyme. Too bad

I won't be around to see it, I add silently. Then, picking up the empty carton, which I'll dump in a trash can somewhere along the road, I roll on out of there as quickly as I can, limping and scratching and grinning like a gorilla that's stolen his arch-enemy's bunch of bananas.

CHAPTER

TWO

or heaven's sake, Wheel. How many times have I told you to begin at the beginning? How in blazes did you come to be dumping fish in somebody's swimming pool in the middle of the night?" That's just what Gramps would be saying if he were in my room right now. Gramps owns the *Marietta Messenger*, our local newspaper, and, like any good reporter, he believes all the important facts of any story should be packed into the first two paragraphs.

It was Gramps who gave me my name. Not my real name, which is Gordon—and which nobody, not even my parents, calls me—but my nickname, which is, of course, Wheel.

To hear him tell the story, when I was a little kid, about five or so, I got a bunch of other kids to take a bunch of their toy cars and arrange them into a perfect parking lot in my room. Then I got them to pay me whatever they had to park their cars there.

The kids didn't seem to mind. But one of them told his mother and she told mine and mine minded a lot. She yelled at me and said I had to give back the dough. Dad, who never yells, tried to explain why what I'd done was wrong. But Gramps, who was visiting at the time, got a big kick out of the whole thing.

"Leave the kid alone. It's about time somebody in this family decided to take after me," he said to my dad, who shut up immediately. "Congratulations, kid. It's the big wheel that makes the mill go round. You've got the makings of a real Big Wheel."

The "Big" got dropped, but the "Wheel" part stuck. And just like Gramps called it, I've lived up to my name. Maybe I haven't made the mill turn, but in my town I've sure made things move. For example, who found two cases of melons that fell off a truck, and who organized the best bowling tournament ever on the Duffys' front lawn—the one with all the plastic flamingos, toadstools, and elves—while they were away on vacation? What person got the gang to dress up as ghosts last Halloween and hit the houses for trick-or-treating, then dump the sheets, smear our faces with charcoal so we looked like hobos, and hit the same houses all over again? I'll give you one guess.

But a mill doesn't have room for two big wheels, and neither does my town. Although that isn't what I was worrying about four weeks ago.

What I was worrying about that sunny afternoon in June, the first day of summer vacation, was what exactly we were going to do for the Fourth of July. I'd promised Tag and the rest of the gang the best holiday ever. Better than last year, when I organized American flag relay races up and down Main Street. Or the year before, when we were a pack of Rollerblading Uncle Sams. So far I hadn't come up with any great ideas, and it was starting to bug me.

But my worrying was interrupted by the doorbell. I went and looked out my window. Tag—my pal, my buddy, my right-hand man—was standing on the porch, one floor below. We go way back, me and Tag. We chucked our training wheels together, lost our baby choppers together, stopped believing in Santa Claus together. Hardly a day went by that I hadn't gone to his place or he hadn't come to mine. The guy's practically a member of the family. He could walk in without ringing anytime. But he's too polite to do that, I thought as I snickered and shook my head. He's too polite to do a lot of things. Or at least he used to be.

I motored out of my room, down the stairs and over to the door. Opening it a crack, I growled, "Who's that *binging* my *rell?*"

There was this silence and then a puzzled voice that said, "It's Tag."

I opened the door wider. "Hey, didn't you listen to Wild Willie this morning?" Wild Willie is our favorite deejay on our favorite radio station, WZIP. He tells crazy stories and does all these funny characters. That day he'd introduced a new one: Migbouth, the tongue-twisted giant.

"Oh yeah. That's right. Guess I was too busy to pay close attention today," Tag said. Now that was weird. Tag always pays attention to Wild Willie. Even weirder was the funny smile he had on his face and the way he was shifting from foot to foot like he either had to go to the bathroom or had some really big news.

"Yeah? What were you busy doing? You couldn't have been studying. School's out," I teased. Tag is what everyone else calls a good student and Gramps calls a grind. It never bothered me that he liked to study. It was kind of like his hobby, I thought. And everybody's entitled to a hobby.

"Going out to the Marietta Mall with my mom." He wiggled around so much I thought he was going to burst.

"The mall? What were you going there for?"

Suddenly he whirled around. "Take a look," he said, pointing to the driveway.

I stepped out onto the porch and looked. There, on the driveway, as usual, was my bike, a three-year-old Tuffy I kept in good condition. I expected to see Tag's wheels next to it—a hand-me-down Quinn so ancient that flakes of rust flew off when he rode it. But instead I saw, sleek, black, and shining, a brand-new, top-of-the-line Lorenzutti.

I flew to it and ran my hand over the smooth leather seat. I was so dazzled that, like a jerk, I asked, "Man, whose is this?"

"It's mine," Tag replied, trotting over to me.

"Yours?"

"Yes. My parents bought it for me because, uh, you know, I did pretty well on my report card." He lowered his voice a little when he said the last part. I guess he didn't want to sound like he was bragging.

I thought he had a right to brag. "Pretty well? You got all A's."

"Not *all*. I got a B+ in science."

"Only because the teacher was a jerk and didn't like your handwriting." I was talking to Tag but still staring at the bike. "Man. Oh man," I whispered, and hopped onto the seat. I closed my eyes and saw myself outracing the locomotive that whizzes past Moorland Park. I got so involved in the daydream, I not only didn't hear a word Tag was saying to me, but I also didn't notice Mike and Corey pull up onto the driveway on their bikes.

Mike and Corey are twins, but they're not identical. Corey's a guy. Mike isn't. Mike's also bigger than her brother, and her hobby's playing drums. If I ever had to fight one of them, I'd pick Corey over Mike any day.

"Wow! A Lorenzutti!" Mike boomed.

My eyes flew open. I had to do a quick maneuver so I didn't fall off the bike.

"When did you get it?" asked Corey.

I hesitated a second before I told them. "It's Tag's."

"Yeah?" They both looked surprised. Then they asked him when and where he got it and about all its features and stuff.

While they talked I kicked up the kickstand and started to ride in slow, wide circles around the driveway. Tag kept looking at me like wasn't I finished riding yet every time I passed him. Each time, I'd smile and wave. Finally, on my fifth pass or so, Mike turned and eagerly asked, "So, what are we going to do today, Wheel?"

That morning I'd been planning to take my gang to the dump. I'd heard that our school had chucked a lot of papers there, and I thought we could go searching for some of next year's tests to have on hand in case we forgot to study. But suddenly, thanks to Tag's new wheels, I had a better idea. But I didn't just blurt it out. That isn't the way I do things.

I braked and put down one foot. However, I didn't get off the bike. I casually looked up at the sky. "Let's see now. Sunny day. High seventy-five to eighty degrees. Wind maybe five miles per hour. Cumulus clouds. Not much chance of rain. I'd say it's a perfect day to test-drive this here Lorenzutti."

"Yeah! All right!" cheered Corey and Mike.

Tag didn't cheer. "I already gave it a test-drive before we bought it."

"Oh. Well. Then we give it a . . . a . . . whaddya call it when you take something on its first real trip?"

"A maiden voyage." Tag always knows stuff like that. He's the only kid I know who reads vocabulary books for fun.

"Yeah. That's it." I grinned at him. "We take it on a maiden voyage."

"Where to?" asked Mike.

"To . . ." I paused. "The Old Wembley Place."

"The Old Wembley Place? Isn't that supposed to be some big run-down house on Beech Tree Road?" asked Corey.

"That's the one," I replied.

Tag looked at me curiously. We'd been to all kinds of places together but never to the Old Wembley Place. He didn't know I'd been there by myself a few weeks ago, when I was supposed to be home sick from school. It wasn't my style to keep things from him. But I was saving the spot for a surprise when the right moment came, and this was the right moment.

"Beech Tree Road is kind of far," he said uncertainly.

"For that old clunker of yours maybe, but this baby can handle it." I tooted the Lorenzutti's horn. I could have come out and asked him if I could ride his bike, but that would have sounded like begging. I didn't like to beg.

"Yeah?" Tag thought about it. "Yeah, I guess you're right." He put his hand on the handlebar.

" 'Course, if you're worried, I'd be happy to ride it there and let you take my trusty old Tuffy." I began to pedal around the driveway again.

When I got back to my bike, I saw Tag getting on it.

"Tracks?" I grinned.

"Tracks," Tag agreed, with a sigh and a chuckle and a shake of his head. He knew I'd tricked him. But he didn't mind. "This had better be good," he said, trying to growl but laughing instead.

"When is one of my ideas ever *not* good?" I said. Then I pointed the bike roadways. "Follow me," I called. "Destination: the Old Wembley Place."

Well, Wheel, you've done it again, I thought as I zipped down the driveway on Tag's new bike, with three members of my gang fanned out behind me. You've come up with another great idea.

And it was a great idea. How was I supposed to know it would also be the start of all my troubles?

CHAPTER

THREE

We picked up the rest of my gang on the way to the Old Wembley Place.

As usual we drew a lot of attention as we rode through town, whistling Wild Willie's theme song. Kwesi was wearing a new red-and-yellow shirt his uncle had sent him from Africa. Brian had on a new Blue Jays baseball cap, which meant that now he was missing only the Mariners and the Expos from his collection. His younger sister Tara had a pair of tap shoes tied by their ribbons around her neck. Brian had tried to get her to leave them home. In fact, as usual, he tried to get her to leave herself at home, and, as usual, she'd refused. And as for Kong, he, of course, had his stuffed gorilla King tied to the back of his bike. Wherever Kong goes, so does King.

People waved to us as we passed: Mrs. Esterhazy, pruning her roses; the Lynches, junior and senior, painting the Peschetti's house; Tom the mailman, making his rounds; the Moscowitz family—all eight of them—waiting at the bus stop; Tag's brother Evan, having a fake fight with his girlfriend, Suzanne, on the library steps. I could tell what each one of them was thinking: "There goes Wheel and his gang off on another great adventure." It made me feel good. Real good.

I didn't feel as good seeing Officer Birdsall, munching his sandwich on a bench by Moorland Park. He and I haven't always seen eye to eye, and I didn't think he'd much approve of our present jaunt. In fact, he'd probably have a nasty name for it, like *trespassing*.

"Hey, Wheel," he called out when he saw me, "you got a permit for this parade?"

"Aw, leave him alone, Bob," said his partner, Officer McPhail. "He's just practicing for the Fourth of July."

I saluted them like a grand marshal. They both laughed, and we rode on, heads high, pedaling faster than ever and whistling louder than before.

But at Beech Tree Road, everybody's voice suddenly got softer, and everybody's bike slowed down. Maybe it was all the fancy mailboxes and marble statues and hedges cut into strange shapes that did it. Or the black gates and the white columns, the long, sweeping driveways, and the trim green lawns. Or just possibly it was because we didn't see a single kid—or hardly even a grown-up—even though it was the middle of the day.

15

"Man, this neighborhood sure is quiet," Tag said, riding beside me.

"You should hear it at night," I told him.

"You've been here at night? Since when?" said Tag. He sounded skeptical, but his eyes were wide.

I grinned. Sometimes it was so easy to fool Tag that I couldn't help myself. And I *was* fooling—then. "Sure," I told him. "Plenty of times."

"No, you haven't," he said. "You must think I'm really gullible."

"You are," I said, and he pretended he was going to ram me with his bike.

"So, where is this place?" Corey called out a few minutes later. He always got tired before anybody else.

"Right here," I said, squealing to a stop at the driveway.

Everybody braked so fast we almost had an eight-bike pileup.

"This is it?" Kong said, in surprise. No one had told him exactly where we were going.

"Ew. It looks icky," said Tara.

She was right. What you could see of the Old Wembley Place—its rusted gates and weed-choked driveway—looked like a scruffy mongrel sitting among a pack of well-groomed poodles. The Wembleys hadn't lived there for years, and neither had anybody else.

"Why can't we go to one of the other houses that look nice?" Tara went on.

16

"Good idea, Tara. Why don't you go ahead and do that—all by yourself," Brian told her.

She ignored him.

"I hope there aren't a lot of bees here," said Kwesi, staring at the weeds. He's allergic to bee stings.

Mike started laughing.

"What's so funny?" he demanded.

She pointed at his colorful shirt. "If you don't want to attract bees, how come you're dressed like a giant tulip?"

"You don't like my shirt?" Kwesi asked, in a warning tone of voice.

"I like it fine, *honey.*" Mike started laughing again.

"We're not going up the driveway," I said, stopping them both. "We're taking the shortcut through the woods. It'll bring us closer to where we want to go. So, come on."

I got everybody to stash their bikes at the turnoff, where nobody could see them. Then I led all of us through the gap in the fence.

The shortcut was easy. Even so, Tara grumbled about how long it was. Corey teased her until he got scratched by a bramble and squealed, "Look, I'm bleeding!" He held out his arm to show a tiny scratch.

I squinted at it. "Hmm, anybody got a microscope?" I asked, and everybody, even Corey, had to laugh.

When we reached the low stone wall at the end

of the path, they all looked at me like "Now, what?"

"Listen up," I said, looking at each one, Tag in particular. "You ready?"

"Ready," he said.

"Good. Over this wall is a row of hedges. Past the hedges is a weedy lawn. On the other side of the lawn is something you'll be glad you came all this way to see."

"What is it?" asked Kwesi.

"Climb over and you'll find out," I told him, scrambling over the wall and disappearing through the hedges.

I couldn't wait to see their faces, especially Tag's. It was fun watching him have fun. And believe me, he wouldn't have had half as much fun in his life if it hadn't been for me.

"There it is," I said, when they'd all joined me at the other side of the lawn.

"A swimming pool?" said Brian.

"An *empty* swimming pool?" Corey put in.

I shook my head slowly. "Nope," I replied, reaching into my pocket and pulling out a small black ball. "Our own private *handball court*."

I looked at Tag. A slow smile spread over his face, like I'd handed him a present. Handball is his favorite game. He's almost as good at it as I am. "Double doubles?" he asked, pulling out his ball.

"Double doubles," I answered. "You and me against Mike and Corey. Brian and Tara against Kwesi and Kong." I tossed my ball to Kong.

18

"Yeah!" everyone whooped, and down into the pool we all went.

Soon the pock-pock of the ball and the pant-pant of our breathing echoed off the peeling blue walls. Mike and Corey played hard and fast. But Tag and I played harder and faster, and we won every single game. Then we played Kwesi and Kong, and we beat them, too.

When we were too tired to play anymore, we climbed out of the pool and stretched out along the edge. The concrete was smooth and warm under our backs. The sun was even warmer on our faces. I could see the rays dancing right through my eyelids.

"This was a great idea, Wheel," said Mike.

"One of your best," Kwesi agreed. "Our own private handball court."

"On our own private estate," I added. "I've got plans for this place. Lots of plans. This is just the beginning."

Tag raised himself on one elbow and looked at me. "But what if somebody else shows up?"

"Who's gonna show up here?" I laughed.

"You never know. Somebody might."

"Yeah," Tara piped up. "Mom says the market's down right now. Somebody could get a good deal on this place and buy it." Brian and Tara's mother sells real estate, and Tara wants to follow in her footsteps.

"Sure," I said, "somebody might buy this place.

19

And someday aliens might land on Main Street."

That started everyone off.

"And someday gremlins might take over the town hall," said Mike.

"And someday Officer Birdsall might grow antlers," Kwesi suggested.

"And next week Kong might be tied to the back of *King's* bike." Brian poked him.

"And on the Fourth of July we'll all do nothing because Wheel won't have a single good idea," said Tag.

Everyone laughed real hard at that one. I laughed loudest of all.

C H A P T E R

F O U R

t's 7:05, 05, 05. If you're alive, alive, alive, Wild Willie says, 'What's your function?' " the voice blared out of the radio.

"I don't know. What's yours?" I hollered back.

A week had passed since I'd shown my gang the Old Wembley Place. We'd been going to the estate every day, playing handball, doing sprints on the unmowed lawn, trying to climb the columns. Today we were going to find a way inside the house. Through the windows we'd seen a wide staircase with banisters that were perfect for sliding races.

The week would have been perfect, too, except for the Fourth of July problem. I still hadn't come up with an idea, and now the holiday was seven days closer. I'd never been stuck for ideas before. It wasn't a good feeling. I was starting to feel irritable. I was beginning to suffer from what Dr. Joyce Brothers calls "executive stress."

Tag had noticed that something was bugging me and wanted to know if maybe I was sick. I had to tell him I was fine. Then he'd wanted to know when I was going to tell him what the Fourth of July plan was. "Soon" was all I'd said. A big wheel's got to act like he always knows where the road is—even around his best friend.

"What do you think I should do, Wild Willie?" I asked now.

"Are you depressed about your life? Are you not living up to your potential? We have the solution," Wild Willie replied. "Just dial 5-5-5-DEDBEAT. Your call will be answered by a lazy, feckless, under-achieving ne'er-do-well who'll make you feel as though you're the hardest-working, most success-ful person in the world. That's 5-5-5-DEDBEAT. Call anytime. We don't have anything better to do."

"Thanks, Wild Willie." I laughed. Then he went into a real commercial. I don't like to miss a single word of Wild Willie if I can help it, so that was a good time to flick off my radio, hurry to the kitchen for breakfast, and turn on the radio in there.

But when I left my room I realized the radio in the kitchen was already on, tuned to the same sta-tion and blasting away at full volume.

I wondered who'd turned it on. I didn't think it was Mom. She not only hates loud radios, but she also hates Wild Willie. She blames him for all the times I was late for school this year. I kept telling her if she'd get me a Walkman I could listen to Wild Willie on the way to school and get there on time.

"Not on your life," she'd reply. "Then you'd be hiding in the last row with those earphones on your head, listening to that deejay instead of to your teacher."

"I wouldn't be hiding in the last row. I'm assigned to row two, and we can't change our seats," I argued. I wasn't about to tell her I would have used my hooded sweatshirt to camouflage the earphones instead.

Anyway, since Mom was letting Wild Willie blast his way into our kitchen it meant one of two things: (a) she'd suddenly figured out what I'd been telling her all along—that Wild Willie is the greatest deejay in the universe, or (b) something was wrong.

It was obvious when I booked into the kitchen that the answer was *b*. Mom was at the stove, whipping around her spatula like she was playing slapjack instead of flipping flapjacks. Only one thing makes her do that. Or should I say one person. And sure enough, there he was at the table, working his way through a big stack of pancakes and yelling at Dad.

"What do you mean you don't have a TV personality? TV stars aren't born. They're made," he boomed, almost as loud as the radio.

"Hey, Gramps," I greeted him. "Find any bombs today?"

It's a joke between us. Last year some crazy woman called Gramps's newspaper and said there was a bomb under the press. Gramps went and found the bomb and dismantled it himself. When he was asked why he didn't call the cops, he said it made better headlines this way. Before the bomb incident, a lot of people had heard of Gramps. Afterward, everyone had.

Gramps turned to me. "Not yet," he replied on cue. "But the day's still young." Then he went right back to bawling out Dad, who was cutting his pancakes into itsy-bitsy pieces and pushing them around on his plate.

"The WPAR job is a plum. A plum! And you won't even send in your résumé!"

"I don't want to argue with you, Pop," Dad said, slicing away with his fork. A piece of pancake flew to the floor.

"Why not? I'd like to hear one good reason besides this TV personality nonsense why you won't go out for this job."

Dad didn't say anything. Gramps went on hollering. And I tuned out. They'd been through this before over Dad's career. What it was about is this: Dad is a meteorologist, which means he studies and forecasts the weather. He can talk about things like cold fronts, air masses, windchill factor, and barometric pressure. He can look at a satellite weather map and tell you if tomorrow will be a good day to get a suntan or whether you'd better not go out without your umbrella, just like the forecasters on TV. Except that Dad has never been on TV. He spends all his time at the weather station, calling in reports to the TV guys. And furthermore, he's happy about it. He says not all meteorologists want to be on TV. Gramps doesn't understand this. Every time he hears about a TV gig, he gets on Dad's case. How could anybody not want to be on the tube, he says. And to tell you the truth, I wonder about that myself.

But I didn't need to hear him tell that to Dad again, so I turned up the radio a little more.

"And now," Wild Willie reverberated through the kitchen, "it's time to play 'What's My Blunder?' Here's Boner Number One:

"I'm setting the table for a formal dinner. I place the steak knife, dinner fork, and salad fork to the right of the plate, the soup and dessert spoons to the left. What's my blunder?"

"Listen, you could be the next Willard Scott," Gramps's voice rose over Wild Willie's. "You take a few acting lessons. You get yourself a new look. And, above all, you get yourself a good agent. I know a few. . . ."

Dad picked up the newspaper, and Mom slammed a plate of pancakes in front of me and growled right into my ear, "Forks on the left, spoons on the right."

"Huh?" I said.

"That's right!" exclaimed Wild Willie. "Forks on the left, spoons on the right. Boner Number Two: My aunt has just had a baby. I take one look at my new cousin and laugh. He looks just like a chimpanzee. 'Wow, what an ugly little monkey,' I say. What's my blunder?"

25

"Grow your hair longer. Maybe a beard," Gramps shouted.

"A chimpanzee isn't a monkey. It's an ape," Mom yelled louder.

"Way to go, Mom!" I cheered. She was amazingly good at this game.

Dad was still reading the same page of the paper—a big ad for ladies' lingerie. I turned the page for him on my way to the radio, which I flicked up another notch just as Tag came into the room, wincing.

"Rang bell . . . nobody . . ." was all I could make out.

"Boner Number Three," Wild Willie resounded. "I've been invited to my ex-girlfriend's wedding. The invitation says it's a white-tie affair. I put on my tuxedo and arrive on time for the ceremony. Just before the bride can say 'I do,' I run up to the altar, punch out the groom, sling the bride over my shoulder, and hustle out the side door. What's my blunder?"

"The trouble with you, Dan, isn't that you don't have a TV personality. It's that you don't have ambition!" Gramps thundered.

"You wear a tailcoat to a white-tie wedding, not a tux!" Mom shrieked, banging her skillet on the stove.

Dad snapped the newspaper and knocked over the maple syrup.

"Maybe . . . bet— . . . leave." Tag turned to go.

I stood up and clapped a hand on his shoulder.

"No need," I said, though I doubt he heard me. Then I took a deep breath, and, in the foghorn voice I save for occasions like this, I blared, "Everybody shut up! Now!"

There was immediate silence. Except, of course, for Wild Willie. "Boner Number Four," he whooped. "Wild Willie is having a contest. The winner gets to meet him and appear live on the Wild Willie Showdown. I didn't enter the contest. What's my blunder?" he said.

"What?" Tag and I looked at each other.

"Beats me," Mom muttered, cleaning up the syrup.

"My blunder is not entering Wild Willie's contest. Don't let it be *your* blunder. Details after this commercial."

"Is he kidding?" Tag was wide eyed. "A chance to meet Wild Willie and be on his show?"

"First I've heard of it," I replied.

"Now there's somebody with a good agent," said Gramps, turning to Dad. But he found himself face-to-face with an empty chair. "Where'd he go?"

"To work," Mom answered. "Where I'll also be going shortly and where you ought to be already."

Gramps lowered his bushy eyebrows. "I'm leaving in a minute. I want to hear more about this contest. I like contests. They make good press."

The commercial ended. There was a big fanfare. Then Wild Willie came back on, "You say you want to meet Wild Willie? You want to pat him on the back, shake his hand, shower him with adulation and lots and lots of bucks? Well, here's your chance. No kidding now. This one's for real. . . ."

"Holy cow!" squeaked Tag. "It's true!" He was leaning out of his chair and panting.

"Calm down," I told him, even though I was just as excited. Then I commanded, "Go on, Wild Willie. Tell us the rules."

He obeyed. "The contest rules are simple. First, grab yourself a postcard." He paused.

"Yes?" Tag said, hanging on every word.

"Second, on that postcard, in twenty-five words or less, tell me about your fabulous plans for . . ." *Da-da-dada-da-dadadadadaDA*, a band played a few bars of the famous march called "Stars and Stripes Forever."

"Oh no," I mumbled, but nobody heard.

"That's right! You guessed it! Tell me what stupendous, supercolossal, funsy-wunsy picnic, party, parade, or other event you have planned for the Fourth of July!" Wild Willie continued. "Then mail the card to me, Wild Willie. You have until June thirtieth to enter. I'll pick the person whose plans I like the best and announce his or her name on July 3 at 8:15 A.M. If you're the lucky winner, you'll receive a Wild Willie jacket and baseball cap and you'll get to appear on my show as cohost for a day! So enter now. Don't delay!"

Fireworks exploded out of the radio, and Tag, who's usually calm as a catfish, leapt out of his seat. He jumped up and bounced around the room, exclaiming, "Wow! Wowie, wow, wow! We're going to meet Wild Willie! We're going to meet the Man!"

"How do you figure that?" I asked, trying to sound casual, as I turned down the volume.

"Because you said we're going to have the best Fourth of July ever, and there's nobody in the world who could possibly have better plans than you!"

"Hmm. 'Local Boy to Host Radio Show,' " said Gramps. "I like it. Good human-interest stuff."

"He'd better start looking for an agent," muttered Mom.

"So, what have you got cooked up for the Fourth of July?" asked Gramps. He was looking at me. So were Mom and Tag.

I took a big swallow of juice and looked back at them all, as coolly as I could. "I can't tell you just yet. There are still a few details to be worked out."

Gramps squinted at me. "Being cagey, huh?" he growled. "Won't let your beloved grandfather have an inside scoop?" Then he wiggled his eyebrows to show he was teasing.

"That's right," I declared steadily, even though I wasn't feeling steady at all. I wiggled my eyebrows back, while in some little room inside me, that nasty executive stress tacked its nameplate on the door, like it was planning to stick around for a while.

CHAPTER

FIVE

Be careful what you wish for. You might get it." I don't know how many times Mom told me that one, but I do know I never believed it.

It's a good thing I never told her what I was wishing for a couple of hours after Wild Willie announced the Fourth of July contest, or she would be shaking her finger at me now, saying, "I told you so." What I was wishing was that my whole gang would disappear.

The thing is they were driving me crazy. They'd all been listening to Wild Willie, every single one of them. And all of them—except for Tag, who was giving me a long-suffering look I couldn't stand—kept asking over and over, as we rode to the Old Wembley Place, what was my big plan for the Fourth of July.

"Is it serious or funny?" asked Mike.

"Do I get to wear a costume?" questioned Tara.

"Did you send off the postcard already?" Kwesi wanted to know.

"And did Tag check your spelling?" teased Kong.

"It's under control," I told them, and it shut them up for awhile, which gave me a chance to think some more. All morning my mind had been working overtime—and not getting paid for it.

But when we began walking up the shortcut, they started in again:

"When are you going to tell us?" asked Corey.

"Does anybody else know?" asked Kong.

"Can I be the star?" Tara demanded.

"What kind of star? The *Dog* Star?" teased Brian, who likes astronomy.

"The star of *what*? He hasn't told us yet what the plan is," said Mike.

"Yeah. So, what *is* the plan?" asked Kwesi.

"When are you going to tell us?"

"What are we going to do?"

"Come on, Wheel. Tell us, Wheel. Tell us. Tell us."

They were surrounding me, as much as I could be surrounded on the narrow path, like the sheep on my uncle Rodney's farm when you walk into their pen with food. They even looked like sheep to me, with long faces and big eyes, and they sounded like sheep bleating, too. And that's when I wished they would all disappear.

But suddenly Corey said, "Hey, what was that?"

We all stopped. "What was what?" I asked.

"That sound. Like something thumping. Didn't you hear it, Kwesi?"

"No," he replied.

"I didn't either," said Tara.

"You couldn't hear anything—you've been clicking your tap shoes together the whole time," Brian told her.

"Maybe it was a bird. A woodpecker," Kong suggested.

"Maybe it was King, back by Kong's bike, beating on his chest," said Mike. She pounded on hers and yodeled. Kwesi and Brian joined in. Everyone laughed.

Except Tag. "I heard it, too," he said. "But it wasn't one thump—it was several. And it came from that direction." He pointed toward the stone wall, with the lawn and the pool beyond.

We all listened again. Nobody heard anything. But there was a sudden chill in the air. The woods, which just a moment before had been friendly and familiar, suddenly seemed dark and fuzzy around the edges. I knew that any minute somebody was going to start talking about ghosts, and someone else was going to say maybe we ought to go some other place today.

I took charge. "Whatever it was—if it was anything—it's gone now," I declared. "Let's play a couple of games of handball and then find a way into the house."

Immediately, everyone fell into line. We climbed the wall and pushed through the hedges onto the wide, empty lawn. "See," I said. "All clear. There's nothing and nobody here." We raced across the grass to the pool.

When we got to the edge, we looked down and stopped dead. There, in the deep end, was a skinny kid wearing a top hat and spinning round and round on a one-wheeled bicycle.

Tara shrieked. Corey yelled, "Holy cow!" The kid fell off his weird bike, and everyone laughed.

He didn't seem to care. He picked himself up quickly, dusted himself off, looked up at us, and grinned. It annoyed me, that grin. It was way too cocky. "Welcome," he said, spreading out his arms wide.

"Who are you?" I demanded. "And what are you doing here? This is private property."

The kid grinned again. "That's right. It *is* private property. But it's okay. I don't mind—and Dad won't either. We like visitors."

"What are you talking about, visitors?" I sneered. "You make it sound like you own this place."

The kid kicked up his top hat with his foot. It sailed up into the air, flipped over twice, and landed neatly on his head. Tara applauded. He bowed to her, then looked back at me. "I do," he said.

"Sure you do," I said loudly. "And my name's Wild Willie." I turned and winked at Tag. He and the rest of my gang laughed.

"Pleased to meet you, Wild Willie," the kid responded. "Should I call you Willie or just plain Wild?"

Tara and Corey giggled. I squinted at them, and they shut up.

"You know how to get out of this pool yourself, or should we show you how?" I threatened.

"Oh, I think I can manage," the kid replied, and, mounting his unicycle, he began to hop it up the steps.

"Man, he's good on that thing," Kwesi murmured.

"He's like this guy I saw at the circus," said Tara.

"Yeah, a real clown," I jeered, glancing at Tag again. But this time he didn't return the glance or laugh. He and the rest of my gang were too busy watching the kid, and that really annoyed me.

By then the show-off had reached the top of the steps. He rode over to us, really close to the edge of the pool. "My name's Topper," he said matter-of-factly, looking at me. "My dad and I are moving here from the city."

"Yeah? And where's he?" I wanted to know.

"He's around."

"Sure he is," I scoffed.

"He's talking to some workmen over by the house. The painters, I think. Or maybe the plumbers."

"How come you're moving here?" asked Mike, suspiciously.

"My dad says the city's getting on his nerves. It's too crowded and dirty and expensive. Here in the country we can save money and live like kings."

"Yeah. This is some palace," I snickered, looking at the cracked swimming pool and the weedy lawn.

"It will be once we get it fixed up," the kid replied. He started doing quarter, then half, jump-turns on the cycle. "Want me to give you a tour?"

"We've already seen this place, right, Tag?" I said. I got out my rubber ball and began tossing it from one hand to the other.

Tag didn't answer. He was watching the kid do his tricks. I gave him a nudge, and he nodded.

"Yeah? But I bet you haven't seen all of it. I bet you haven't been inside the house. There are some great banisters there for sliding, and there's a really spooky attic." The kid stopped jumping and looked at Tara.

"We saw the banisters through the windows. Wheel was going to get us inside the house after we played handball in the pool."

"Who's Wheel?"

"He is." She pointed to me.

"I thought he was Wild Willie," the kid said, all innocent, and he started doing those jump-turns once more.

I tossed my ball harder. It aimed itself at the kid's head. He caught it and finished a one-hundred-and-eighty-degree jump at exactly the same time.

"How'd you get so good at that?" Kwesi asked.

"Practice," the kid replied. "I'm good at handball, too. I'll play with you. We've got enough time before the repairmen come to fix the pool."

"You're going to fix up the pool?" I blurted, stunned. Up till then I hadn't believed him about owning the house. But suddenly I had this sinking feeling maybe he was telling the truth.

"Sure. Then we can fill it, which is what you usually do with swimming pools, right, Tag?" He shot his eyes at him and then back at me with that big grin.

That really pulled my chain. "We don't feel like playing handball anymore. We've got other things to do," I said coolly, holding out my palm for the ball.

Suddenly his face kind of fell a little.

For a moment I actually felt sort of sorry for him. Whoever he was, he was there all by himself, without any friends, without any gang. If he really is moving here, he'll be kind of lonely, I thought. The city's pretty far away. Then he looked me in the eye and said, "Yeah? Like what?"

"What do you mean, like what?" I asked, confused.

"What other things have you got to do?"

Then and there my mind went blank—as blank as it had been so far about the Fourth of July. I couldn't think of an answer. I couldn't think of anything at all. I heard my gang shuffling behind me, waiting for me to say something, anything.

"We have lots of things to do," I heard Tag prompt me. But his voice sounded far away, like he was across a lake. I didn't look at him. Neither did Topper. I just kept standing there, staring at the kid, with my hand held out, and he kept staring back at me, holding my ball in his fingertips, like a freeze-frame in a movie.

I don't know how long we would've stayed that way if a man hadn't appeared, saying, "Heck, Topper, I leave you alone for an hour and what happens? You make eight new friends."

The kid gave a little twitch and tossed me my ball. I caught it and stuck it in my pocket.

"I've got some Cokes in the kitchen—or what will be a kitchen. Anybody want any?" The man smiled at me. He was an ordinary-looking guy—brown hair, brown eyes, not tall or short, fat or thin. I felt like there was something familiar about him, but what I couldn't say.

"They're just leaving, Dad," the kid said.

"Oh? That's too bad. Tell you what, though. We're going to have a big bash here on the Fourth of July. If you guys—and gals—have nothing to do, why don't you come?"

"Thank you," I said, politely. "But we're going to be very busy."

"Having a picnic?" the man asked.

Suddenly I felt everyone looking at me. And I also felt something pecking inside my skull, like a chick trying to break out of an egg. I shut my eyes.

I was a little dizzy, and I was starting to sweat. I wanted to get out of there really bad. "No!" I said, or maybe shouted, opening my eyes.

The man's eyebrows were raised. The kid was staring at me with his forehead furrowed. Behind me, I heard my gang muttering.

Then all of a sudden, my head was clear—but far from blank. Yes! Hooray! Eureka! Bingo! I felt like shouting, leaping, wriggling on the ground like a slaphappy puppy. "No," I repeated, calmly, instead. "No, we're not having a picnic. We're having a . . . carnival. The biggest, best carnival our town has ever seen, put on by me and my gang!"

I grinned at the man, at the kid, at everybody around me. "Wow! Yeah! All right!" my gang exploded. Tag was smiling so wide even his freckles were grinning. I held up my hand to quiet everyone. "And the best part . . . the best part is going to be our emcee. Maybe you've heard of him."

"Who is he?" the man asked.

"His name is Wild Willie, and he's the greatest deejay on the radio!"

"Wild Willie?" The man gave his son a funny look. "I don't think I've heard of him. Have you, Topper?"

"Yeah," the kid answered. "He's nothing much." Now I knew for certain the guy was a jerk.

"Well, I'll have to listen to him sometime," the man said. "So, Topper, I've got something I want to show you in the cellar. Let's vamoose."

"Okay." The kid turned to me. "See you around, Wheel."

I nearly made a goon face at him, but that's baby stuff. So I just waved to let him know he wasn't going to bother me—not now, not ever. Then he and his dad left.

When they were out of sight, I quietly started humming "Stars and Stripes Forever." Tag, giving me the thumbs-up, joined in, followed by Kwesi, Mike and Brian, then Tara and Corey, and last of all, Kong, with his deep, off-key voice. As we marched back to our bikes, humming so loud I thought they could hear us back in town, I felt like a general leading his troops home in victory after winning a war. Little did I know that all I'd won was the first battle.

CHAPTER

SIX

Boreas," Dad said, twirling his new camel-shaped weather vane, with a blank look on his face.

"Huh?" I said. It was a couple of hours after my brilliant brainstorm at the Old Wembley Place. Tag and I were up on my roof, where I'm only allowed to be when Dad is putting up one of his seventeen— excuse me, eighteen—weather vanes.

He loves those vanes. Every one of them is different. He's got a dog weather vane, a cat weather vane, a horse, an airplane, a spaceship, several kinds of birds, and even one that looks like a midget pterodactyl! He spends a lot of time polishing them, adjusting them, and standing around watching them point out the direction the wind's blowing—as if they're some great TV show he doesn't want to miss. Mom says it's his form of relaxation. It calms him down. Which makes no sense to me. If my dad got any calmer, he'd be in hibernation.

Anyway, for as long as I could remember he'd put up a different weather vane on the first day of the month. The fact that the first day of the month was three weeks away should have told me right then and there that something was out of whack. But I was too pumped up to notice, and also too bugged. I'd just told Dad about my sensational Fourth of July plans, and what did I get back? Some gobbledlygook about Boreas that I didn't even understand!

Dad spun the vane in the opposite direction. "Zephyrus . . ." He looked up. "The Greeks."

"The Greeks?" said Tag.

"The Greeks believed there were eight winds, and they gave each one a name and a personality. Boreas is the north wind, Zephyrus is the west."

"So that's where the word *zephyr* comes from!" said Tag.

"Yes. And *boreal*—"

"Jeez," I growled, hurling an acorn off the roof like I was trying to throw out a runner at first. "I just tell you about the amazing, supercolossal extravaganza I'm planning for the Fourth of July, and you're talking about hot air." I glared at Dad—and Tag, too, even though I thought he was just doing his usual polite thing. Tag hunched his shoulders and dropped them to apologize. Dad focused his eyes on me like he was reading a rotating beam ceilometer.

"I'm sorry, Wheel," he said, like he meant it. "You know I like to hear about your plans. I'm just a little distracted today."

"A little?"

"Well, maybe more than a little." He smiled. "Tell me your news again. I'll try to pay attention this time." He leaned against the chimney with his arms folded.

"Okay." So I started all over again. I was on a roll, too, hatching ideas left and right in my head about the carnival, like what kind of acts we'd have and who was going to do what. Dad was nodding and Tag was adding a couple of comments here and there, telling me what sounded good and what didn't. But soon I saw Dad's eyes begin to glaze over, like the long-winded Greeks were blowing through his brain again, and I was ready to tell him forget it—if he wasn't interested, I knew Gramps would be—when Mom's head popped up at the top of the ladder.

"Well, it looks like this is where the action is." She hoisted herself up onto the roof and studied the camel weather vane. "I don't know why, but this one makes me want to reach for a cigarette."

"But Mrs. Wiggins, you don't smoke," said Tag.

"Maybe that's why I can never find a cigarette when I reach for one." She laughed. Tag looked confused. Then Mom turned to me. "Had a good day, Wheel?"

"Yeah. I was just telling Dad about it—for the *second* time," I said. I started to tell her about the carnival, and she listened for about thirty seconds before her eyes did their glassy number. Then she turned to Dad and said, "Your boss just called again."

Dad picked a cinder off his shirt absentmindedly. "You know, Wheel, there was a waterspout over the Mississippi today down in New Orleans," he said, staring somewhere over my left ear.

I stopped trying to talk about my plans and looked at him, confused.

"I told him you'd call him back shortly," Mom went on.

Dad acted like he hadn't heard her—or didn't want to. "Most unusual, a waterspout over the Mississippi. Over the ocean, not so rare. But over the Mississippi . . ." He rubbed the cinder through his hair. "Most unusual."

"Look, Dan, I'm not like your father," said Mom. "I'm not trying to push you to do something you don't want to do."

Dad kept rubbing his head, harder.

"But I think you do owe Lars an answer soon so they can get someone else if you refuse."

So, okay, I admit it. Once in a while I'm a little slow. Not often, mind you. But this time, yeah. It took me until then to realize something serious was going on. Tag looked at me like he was Dr. Watson. But I couldn't make like Sherlock Holmes and tell him what was afoot because I didn't have a clue. "What are you guys talking about?" I finally blurted out.

"Dan?" Mom asked.

Dad shrugged, as if to say, "Go ahead. Tell him."

"You know Linda Temple, the weatherwoman on WURP?" Mom began.

"Sure, we know who she is," I glanced at Tag. "What about her?"

"Well, she got an offer at another TV station, and she's leaving at the end of the month. There's a new meteorologist lined up for her job, but she's not available until July seventh. . . . "

Suddenly it was as if the foreign movie I'd been watching got translated into English. I understood why Mom's mind wasn't on my plans and why Dad was putting up a new weather vane three weeks early. "They want Dad to fill in for her until then, right?"

"Right," said Mom.

"Wow!" I yelled. "TV! You'll be on TV—and for the Fourth of July! That's got to be one of the most important forecasts of the year. Everybody glued to their sets, waiting for you to tell them whether or not it's gonna rain on their barbecue, picnic, pool party, parade. . . . You'll be famous!"

"I'm not sure I want to be famous, Wheel," Dad said. He tried to lean against the chimney again and missed.

Tag grabbed him before he slipped. "Take it easy, Mr. Wiggins . . . and take your time."

I frowned at Tag. Telling Dad to take his time was like telling a tortoise to slow down.

"Sure you do, Dad. Sure you want to be famous.

Everybody does. And besides, you'll never know for sure if you want to be famous unless you try it."

Dad scoured his head so hard he winced and looked down at his hand. A clump of his hair was sitting in it. He blew it away. It sailed toward our big old maple tree. "Notus," he murmured, "the south wind." He gave a windy little sigh.

"Come on, Dad. Say you'll do it," I urged. "Reach for the stars! Shoot for the moon! Grab the brass ring!" We were all looking at him: me, Mom, Tag.

He cleared his throat and cleared it again. "Well . . . I guess I'll . . . I'll give it a shot."

"Hot dawg and boola-boola!" I cheered, the way Gramps does. "Gramps is gonna go bananas!"

"Maybe we could put off telling him for a while," Mom suggested.

"And let somebody else scoop him? Then he'd *really* go bananas. Right, Dad?" I said.

"You're probably right." Dad sighed. Then he began fiddling with the weather vane again.

"Make sure you give us a good forecast for Independence Day!" I told him.

Five minutes later, I was on the phone giving Gramps the hot news about how his son and his grandson were going to turn all three of us into one power-packed trio of big wheels.

C H A P T E R

S E V E N

"Ice-cream sodas all around," I said, slapping a twenty-dollar bill on the counter of Tucker's Toothsome Delights. The money was mine. The idea was Gramps's.

"If you want people to work hard for you, be a little generous, go a little easy on 'em at first . . . before you crack the whip." That was one of the tips he'd given me the night before on the phone.

"You sure you can afford this?" Tag looked concerned.

"Sure I'm sure," I said. The truth was the twenty just about cleaned me out. But I figured it would be worth it. I would soon be cracking that whip, all right, and I wanted everybody good and ready to giddyap when I did. I grinned confidently at the new waiter, whose nametag said Neil. "Chocolate sodas," I told him.

"I want strawberry," Tara piped up.

46

"Then why don't you go home and ask Mom to make it for you?" said Brian. "Here it's chocolate or nothing."

"I can have strawberry here if I want to, can't I, Wheel? You don't want me to go home, do you? You *invited* me here today so you can tell me what *I* get to do in the carnival." She tossed her head at her brother.

"That couldn't have been Wheel. It must have been a replicant from outer space pretending to be Wheel," Kong teased.

"So, you kids gonna make up your mind or not?" asked Neil. "I haven't got all day."

I turned to him slowly and gave him a smile like hot fudge over ice-cold vanilla. "What time is it?" I finally asked.

"There's a clock right over there. Can't you read it? It says 2:33."

"Uh-huh. And what time do you get off work here?" I queried, sweet and smooth as whipped cream, tilting my chair back as far as I could without tipping it over.

"Closing time, ten o'clock. . . . Hey, what is this? An inquisition?" He looked behind me and my gang for another customer to serve, but there wasn't any.

"If it's 2:33 and you don't leave until ten, then you *do* have all day—and part of the night," I told him, popping the maraschino cherry on my hot-fudge grin. "Now, we'll have seven chocolate sodas and one strawberry, and make it snappy." I shot my seat upright with a spine-tingling crack.

Tag made an imaginary mark on a scoreboard and pointed to me.

Bobby, the other counter guy, who's been there forever, snorted. "That'll teach you not to mess with Wheel, Neil," he said, winking at me.

Steaming, Neil went off to work on our order.

"See? I told you Wheel would let me have whatever I want," Tara said. "I'll bet he'd even buy me that candy troll. Right?"

I nodded. "Wrong," I said at the same time. "Candy trolls are number two on Wild Willie's list of Things I Wouldn't Give a Three-Dollar Bill For."

"What's number one?" asked Kwesi.

"A pack of Olympic shot-putter trading cards."

My gang laughed—except for Corey, who didn't know what a shot-putter was until Tag explained it to him.

We took a table by the window. I waited until Neil, with a scowl, brought us our sodas, and we each had a satisfying slurp. "Okay," I said, glancing slowly around the table till I had everyone's attention. "It's carnival time!"

"All right!" cheered Corey.

"Lay it on us, man," said Kong, with a phony British accent that made us all giggle.

"What makes a good carnival?" I went on. It was what Gramps calls a "rhetorical question," meaning I already knew the answer.

"Good food," answered Brian.

"Good games," said Mike.

"Yeah," added Corey, "like rat race, ringtoss, and bash the bottles."

"Good acts," Tara declared. "A carnival has to have really good acts."

"You're all correct," I said. "Besides food and games, which we'll have to get some of the other kids and their parents to help run, we're going to have a fabuloid show with—what was that word, Tag?"

"*Splendiferous*," he said.

"Yeah, the most splendiferous carnival acts anybody's ever seen!"

"Excellent!" Corey yelled.

"Simply ripping," said Kong, in the same British voice.

Everyone cracked up. Ice cream dribbled out of Brian's nose.

"Hey, that can be his act," said Kwesi. "Brian— the Human Faucet."

"Ugh," said Tara. "Who'd want to see that?"

"A plumber might," said Mike, which made Brian's nose leak again.

Tag handed Brian a napkin, and I said, "Before I tell you about this stupendous show, there's another thing a good carnival needs that nobody bothered to mention."

"What?" asked Kwesi. He had a big ice-cream mustache because he wasn't using a straw. He thought straws were wasteful and bad for the environment. But he couldn't convince me to stop using them. I thought ice cream all over my face was bad for the environment, too.

I took a sip of my soda. "Good publicity," I answered him.

"Oh. Yeah. Where are we going to get that?" asked Corey.

"Wheel's grandpa, dummy," Mike told him. She looked at me. "Right?"

"Right. He's going to give us all the free publicity we can use in his paper, and he'll make sure to mention that we're having a famous mystery guest emcee."

I looked all around the table. Everyone was grinning and nodding—except Kwesi, who said, like he'd been thinking about it for a while, "But you don't know whether or not Wild Willie is really gonna be our emcee because you don't know if you're really gonna win the contest."

"Come off it, Kwesi," said Brian. "You know Wheel's going to win it."

"Yeah, who could possibly come up with a better idea than his?" agreed Mike.

They all looked at me hopefully. "I'll win it. Don't you worry," I vowed, looking back at each of them in turn, Tag last of all. He didn't have a flicker of doubt in his eyes. He trusted me. I felt a twinge of guilt. Because what I hadn't told him was that Gramps was also going to give me some help in that department. He was going to arrange to do an interview with Wild Willie for the *Marietta Messenger* and bring me along as his cub reporter, and nobody, not even Tag, was coming with us.

"This way you can ask him in person to be your

emcee," he'd said. "If anyone can convince Wild Willie, you can. You could sell a pair of water skis to Santa Claus."

"You can really get an interview with Wild Willie?" I'd asked, amazed.

"You bet. You show me a celebrity who doesn't want his name in the paper, and I'll show you a politician who won't kiss babies." Then Gramps said the Wild Willie scheme was just between the two of us. "Otherwise, all your pals will want to come along, and that won't do."

So that was why I was playing mum's the word with my gang when I really felt like letting loose with pop goes the weasel. It was especially hard not telling Tag. But I thought there were some missions a captain couldn't even confide to his first officer, and this was one of them.

Then Tara, who was bouncing around in her seat, burst out, "So, what are the acts?"

"Glad you asked," I said. I stood up and, in a barker's voice, announced, "Step right up, ladies and gentlemen, boys and girls. Step right up for a once-in-a-lifetime thrill. . . ."

"Hey, you. Sit down!" Neil squealed. "This is a restaurant, not a tircus cent . . . I mean circus tent."

"Hey, it's Migbouth," said Brian.

"Man, you a Wild Willie fan, too?" Kwesi called.

I ignored Neil and went on, "Hurry, hurry, hurry. See feats that will astound you, dazzling deeds of derring-do. She's got legs of iron, arms of

51

steel. . . . Come see Mike, the Strongest Girl in America. . . ." I looked at her. She gave a big, delighted grin. ". . . and her assistant, Corey."

He cocked his head like he wasn't sure he'd heard right. "Assistant?" he asked.

I thought he might be less than pleased, and I was ready for him. "Yes, it's a very important job. It's the top-notch assistant that makes the act, and you're going to *top* top-notch."

"Oh," said Corey.

I slapped his back and went into my barker bit again. "Come marvel at Madman Kong, the Gorilla Wrestler, subduing a creature twice his size, and Kwesi the Confounding, Magician Extraordinaire, with a million tricks up his sleeve," I continued, pointing at each of them. Kong snickered. Kwesi frowned. I rolled on. "Come be amazed by Tara, the Tattooed Tap-Dancing Wonder, and Belching Brian, who can recite the entire Pledge of Allegiance in one burp. . . ."

"But I'll look funny with tattoos," Tara interrupted.

"You'll look great with tattoos, Tara. You can have stars, stripes, roses, unicorns—anything you want."

"Anything?" she said.

"Anything." I smiled at her. Then I noticed Brian looking worried. "And besides, they wash off," I added quickly, and he gave a sigh of relief.

Next it was Kwesi's turn to object. "Uh, Wheel,

I'd like to be a magician. But the problem is I don't know millions of tricks. All I know is one. And it comes out of my pocket, not my sleeve."

"Don't worry. You'll learn more. You've got a whole three weeks," I told him.

"Yeah. I guess that's true."

"You bet it is." We slapped five. Out of the corner of my eye I saw Tag waiting patiently. I threw him a quick smile. "And last, but not least, our star attraction . . . ," I announced, and paused.

"What is it?" everybody but Tag asked.

"Our star attraction is . . . ," I repeated, "Wheel and Tag, the Daredevil Bikers! See them jump! See them spin! See them loop the loop the loop!" Now I gave Tag a big grin.

He blinked, and blinked again. He opened his mouth and closed it a couple of times, like a guppy. Then at last he cleared his throat and said, "Can I . . . uh . . . talk to you for a minute, Wheel?"

"Sure," I said, letting him lead me over by the waiter's water station. "Surprised, huh?"

"Yeah, I'm surprised all right. That isn't what we talked about doing yesterday. You know, the Tremendous Tumblers?"

"I know. I came up with this new idea this morning. And it's better, a lot better. Believe me."

"I don't know, Wheel. The thing is . . . uh . . ." He took a deep breath. "I don't think I'm good enough on my bike to be a daredevil biker."

"You will be—with practice. We'll work real hard

on it, and I promise you'll be great, especially on your Lorenzutti." I gave him a little punch on the arm and started back toward the table.

"Uh, wait," he said. I turned back to him, "That's another thing."

"What is?"

"The Lorenzutti. My bike. If we . . . if I mess up, it could get wrecked."

"You won't mess up, and it won't get wrecked. Look, I thought you'd like this. I came up with it just for you and me," I said, a little annoyed that he wasn't so hot on my new idea. But then Tag almost always had to be coaxed, so I forgave him and said, "Trust me. You're gonna be swell. *We're* gonna be swell." I held up my hand for a high five, which he returned, only it felt more like a four. But it didn't bother me. I figured I'd convince him later.

Then we went back to the table, where I was going to deliver my last high-class piece of news about my dad's upcoming TV career.

But my gang was looking out the window. "What about him?" asked Tara. "Is he going to be in our carnival, too?"

I followed all their eyes. There, on the other side of the street in front of the hardware store, was that kid Topper. He was juggling three cereal boxes and attracting a crowd that was growing bigger every moment. But he wasn't looking at them. He was looking across the street—right straight at me.

CHAPTER

EIGHT

The kid saw me watching him back through Tucker's window and dropped one of his cereal boxes. I snickered, thinking he wasn't such a hotshot after all, until I noticed that the box had landed smack in the grocery bag sitting on the side-walk, and bip-bop, it was followed by the other boxes one-twoing it neat and sweet right after. "Show-off," I sneered.

A couple of people dropped some coins into the bag. The kid—Topper—fished a few of them out. Then he gave them, along with what looked like some instructions, to a girl who'd been watching his show. She headed into the hardware store, and he headed across the street toward me.

The way he swaggered into Tucker's like a gun-slinger from a corny old western and plunked him-self at my table, I was afraid for a minute his dad had bought this joint, too, along with the Old Wembley Place. But I knew that was ridiculous, especially when Neil called out, "Hey, you. You gonna order something? You can't sit here unless you order something."

I knew that was bull. Lots of times Dad, who doesn't like ice cream, would sit there with Mom and me and not eat, but I wasn't about to let on to Topper. I wanted his company the way a camper wants a rattlesnake in his tent.

The kid wasn't fazed. He smiled at him. "I'll have what they're all having."

"They're having chocolate. I'm having strawberry," Tara told him.

"That sounds good," he said and grinned at her.

I slurped up the rest of my soda and thought the kid had better be planning to pay for his because I sure wasn't planning to treat.

"Anybody want seconds?" he said, taking out a fancy leather wallet that most kids I know wouldn't be caught dead owning.

"Sure," said Corey.

"No," I blocked. "We don't have time. We've got a lot of work to do."

Corey tsked. Kwesi and Brian grumbled. But Mike said, "Wheel's right. We have to practice for the carnival."

"Right, the carnival. Actually, I've been wanting to talk to you about that," Topper said

"Yeah?" I asked, tapping my straw against my

empty glass. I was a little surprised, but I didn't show it.

"Yeah. I've decided I want to be part of it." Topper smiled again, like he was real proud of himself.

"Well, isn't that something? You *decided* that, huh?" I smiled back. Out of the corner of my eye I could see Tag squinting at the kid and tapping his straw the way I was. "What have you *decided* you want to do? Sell food? Run one of the games?"

Topper gave me a look of disbelief. "No. I want to perform." I heard his "of course," even though he didn't add it. "I can ride my unicycle and juggle—as you may have noticed." He puffed out his chest like a bullfrog who thinks he's king of the pond.

"Oh yeah? Yeah, I guess I did notice. You're pretty good, too," I said.

The kid looked so genuinely pleased I hesitated for maybe five seconds before I chased him off his lily pad. "Too bad we don't need you," I said.

Topper frowned like he hadn't heard me right. "You're telling me I can't be in the carnival?"

"That's right. We've got all the acts we need."

"But Wheel . . . ," Corey began.

"He's *good*," said Tara at the same time.

I shot them both a look. They shut up. But they kept frowning. There was a kind of tension in the air I didn't like. Then Neil brought the kid's soda and plopped it on the table so hard some of the fizz slopped over the side of the glass into Tara's lap.

"Hey, watch it!" yelled Brian, handing his sister a napkin.

"What's the matter with that guy?" said Mike, as Neil walked away.

"Maybe he needs Flip-a-Sack," Tag said calmly, and blew bubbles into his soda.

It was a good move—breaking the tension and pulling us together the way we should have been—and I grinned my appreciation at him. "Do you feel tired and grumpy?" I went into the Wild Willie routine. "When people say, 'Good morning,' do you snap, 'What's so good about it?' "

Kong picked it up, "Do you swear at those TV commercials featuring people perking up over orange juice . . ."

"Tingling over toothpaste . . . ," Kwesi continued.

"Singing in the shower?" Mike put in.

"Then you need Flip-a-Sack—the handy-dandy device for people like you who get up on the wrong side of the bed," Brian announced.

"Just one touch of the button, and Flip-a-Sack's patented rotisserie action rolls you gently, but firmly, over to the right side of the bed," I went on, looking at Tag. He joined in with, "You'll wake up full of vim, vigor, and vo-dee-o-do."

Then everybody chorused, "Flip-a-Sack—the best way to start your day."

"Batteries not included," I concluded, and we slapped five all around the table.

"You'll have a better chance of getting Wild Willie as your emcee with me in the show," Topper said.

I whipped my head around. For a moment I'd forgotten the kid was still there. "What did you just say?" I asked, not believing how nervy this guy was.

"I said you'll have a better chance of getting Wild Willie as your emcee with me in the show," he repeated. His voice was quiet, but it rang in my ears like a broken alarm clock going off at six A.M. on a Sunday morning. And it ticked me off something fierce.

"Oh yeah? Well, that's a shame because I already entered the contest, and I didn't happen to mention *your* name in the entry," I said, shoving back my chair and standing up.

My gang stood up, too—some of them a little slower than they should have.

"It's been real, Neil," I called out and headed for the door, with everyone but Topper following.

We were out on the street when I saw the kid's dad coming toward us from the hardware store. "Hi. Wheel, isn't it?"

"Yeah, that's right," I replied.

"Topper isn't with you? He sent a message he was going to the ice-cream parlor with you guys."

"He's still there," I said, nodding my head toward Tucker's. I didn't want to keep talking to this guy who made the place sound like my great-grand-ma's living room.

"Oh." Mr. Topper, or whatever his name was, looked a little surprised.

"He wants to be in our carnival, but Wheel told him no," said Tara.

"Oh," the guy said again, studying me for a moment. If he thought I was going to explain myself, he had another think coming. "Well. I guess I'll go join him for a soda." He walked away into the shop.

"What did you tell him that for?" Brian bawled out Tara.

"Because it's true." She shrugged.

"You know," said Corey, "I think Topper would be good in our show."

"Forget it," I told him. "The guy's got a large hat size."

"Yeah," said Kwesi, "but he's still good."

"I said forget it," I snarled so loudly that every-body stared at me in silence. I would have stared at me, too. The kid had gotten to me more than he should have, and I wasn't sure why. I forced myself to laugh. "I mean, telling us we need *him* to win the contest. The guy's not even a Wild Willie fan. Remember the other day? He said Wild Willie was *nothing much*. He probably wants to mess us up so we'll look stupid in front of Wild Willie. Right, Tag?"

Tag didn't hesitate. "Wheel's right," he said. "The guys an egotist. We don't need him."

"No, we don't," Brian, Mike, and Kong agreed.

All of a sudden, everything was okay again. I felt good. I felt full of vim, vigor, and vo-dee-o-do. "Trust me. We're going to win this contest all by ourselves, and the carnival's going to be great! Really great!"

"Yeah!" everybody—or almost everybody—declared. Tara was too busy sucking on a candy troll, though how and when she got it, I didn't know. I shook my head at her, and we took off for the park to rehearse.

C H A P T E R

N I N E

Here's a little trick I call 'Egg-ceptional,' " Kwesi said wearily. "Watch closely." He pulled a chicken puppet out of his sleeve and held it over a derby, which was sitting on a black-draped table in his backyard. "Cluck, cluck," the puppet said, and started to lay eggs. The first two rolled out slowly, the way they were supposed to. But the next three popped out like gumballs from a vending machine gone berserk. One landed in the hat, one on the table, and one splattered on Kwesi's shoe.

"Maybe he needs a different chicky-chicky-chicken," said Tara, tap dancing the last phrase.

"Or a bigger hat," said Mike. With a grunt she dropped her barbell, which Corey promptly tried to clean and jerk. But he wiped out instead.

"Wheel . . . ," Kwesi complained.

"Keep on going. Big finish," I told him.

He sighed and picked up his magic wand. "Alakazim, alakazam, alakazalaka, make the eggs scram!" He grabbed the hat and put it on his head with a toothy smile that faded fast as slimy yolk oozed from under the brim and trickled down his face.

"Told you he couldn't do it," Brian said to Corey. "That'll be three Mars bars delivered to my door tomorrow at ten."

"I think he ought to call this trick 'No *Eggs*-it,' " said Kong.

"Wheel!" Kwesi roared.

"Do it again," I said calmly.

He stared at me. "You've got to be kidding! I've already done it five times today. If I use up all my mom's eggs, she'll kill me."

"I'll buy her some more. Do it again. It'll get better."

"It won't get better. It'll get worse. I can't do it. It's too hard. Let me look at the magic book and find an easier trick."

"No. An easier trick won't impress the audience the way this one will," I explained.

"Bet he could make one of Brian's Mars bars disappear," Kong kidded.

"Ha-ha," Kwesi laughed humorlessly.

"I think he already has," said Mike, pointing at Kwesi's pudgy stomach.

"You should talk, Big Boody . . . I mean, Buddy," Kwesi retorted.

"Maybe we should take a break," Tag suggested.

"We already had a break," I argued.

"I think we need another one," Tag insisted.

"Okay. All right." I gave in. "Take five." Everybody but me and Tag collapsed all over Kwesi's grass. I went over to the hose and took a long drink. Then I ran the water over my head. "You want some?" I asked Tag.

He nodded, and Brian stifled a giggle, thinking I was going to do the old thumb spray number on him. But I just handed over the hose without giving Tag even one little squirt. If I started fooling around, everybody else would, and we didn't have time for that. Not if we wanted to look good in front of our folks, friends, neighbors, and especially our emcee, whom I was beginning to worry about getting.

Gramps had called Wild Willie's office several times to set up the interview. All his secretary had told Gramps was that Wild Willie was very busy and she'd get back to him as soon as something opened up.

"It'll happen," Gramps told me. "Don't worry. And, remember, don't tell anybody."

"I won't," I'd said, which was the truth, as far as his second don't went.

"Maybe you should let him do a different one," Tag was saying in a low voice.

"Huh?" I blinked. I hadn't been listening. "What? What are you talking about?"

"That egg trick. Maybe Kwesi's right. Maybe it *is* too hard."

"How could it be too hard? I got it out of *The Perfect Prestidigitator's Guide to 99 Tricks You Too Can Do.*"

Tag shrugged.

"He'll get it. You'll see."

Tag didn't say anything. I grabbed the hose from him and took another drink.

From the other side of the yard, Tara whined, "It's hot."

"Yeah," Corey agreed. "Why don't we go swimming?'

"The town pool's too crowded," Mike said.

"We can go see if that Topper's pool is full yet. If it isn't, we can play in his attic. He told me he's got an excellent attic, with a trunk of old clothes and stuff," said Tara.

"He does?" said Kwesi.

They all looked at me.

I felt a muscle in my cheek give a startled little twitch. Topper. Even when he wasn't around, his name kept coming up like a bad jingle nobody could stop singing. Keeping my voice cool, I said, "Yeah? When did he say that?"

"Yesterday. When we saw him at the baseball card store. Right, Brian?"

"Yeah," Brian admitted. "He wanted to know how the carnival was going, and I said it was going good."

"Except for Kwesi's magic act and Brian's gross burping and I still think I'll look dumb in those tattoos," Tara added.

"I already told you, you'll look great," I said as usual.

But this time it didn't work. "I'll look *dumb*," she insisted.

"Did that kid tell you that when you told him about the carnival?" I nearly growled.

"No. He just laughed. Then he bought Brian a Jose Canseco rookie card."

"Yeah?" said Kong, surprised.

We both turned to Brian. He gave a kind of embarrassed shrug.

"Topper's pool would feel great right now," said Corey. "If it's full."

"Yeah," said Kwesi. "It would."

I got really bugged then. The carnival was a big deal and my gang knew it. Or at least they should have. Instead all they could think about was that kid and his pool. It was like he'd hypnotized them or something.

Well, I was going to have to shake them out of that trance. If being gung ho, here we go, didn't do it, I'd try a different way. "It's okay to speak softly and carry a big stick," Gramps told me, "except when you have to speak loudly." I figured it was time to raise my voice.

"Break's over," I said. "Everybody back to work."

Tara and Corey and Kwesi grumbled. Kong claimed his gorilla was staging a sit-down strike. Brian said, "All work and no play makes Jack a dull boy" on one burp. Mike got up, hefted her barbell, and told them they were a bunch of wimps.

I looked over at Tag. He was frowning. "You gonna complain, too?" I demanded.

"No," he said quietly.

"Good. Because you and I haven't even *begun* to practice yet." I turned back to Kwesi. "Okay, let's see that trick again. As they say in show biz, 'Take it from the top.' "

Rehearsal was over, and I was thinking about jackets. Red or maybe white, with gold lettering that spelled "Daredevils." I could probably wangle a couple of them out of Gerber's Good Sports if I let Mr. Gerber advertise for free in our program, which Mr. Jonas was printing, also for free, to pay off a long-standing debt he owed me for pretending it was my handball instead of his that accidentally jammed the press one day.

"What do you think we should wear in our act," I asked Tag, as we rode to my place, "red jackets or white?"

"I don't know," Tag said, like he also didn't care.

"What's the matter with you?" I asked.

"Nothing. Just tired I guess. We worked hard."

"Yeah," I agreed. "And it paid off. You got it. You got the Standing Double Wheelie."

"Yeah. I did, didn't I?" He perked up a little.

"You sure did. You were great! Next time we'll move on to the harder stuff."

"The harder stuff?"

"Yeah. The Reverse Ramp Twist. The Grand

Handstand. The Vault of Death. Stuff like that."

"The Vault of Death?" Tag stared at me.

"Hey, watch out!" I yelled.

He whipped his head around and swerved, just missing Mrs. Creamer's fat and lazy cat, Bony.

"Don't worry," I said. "It sounds harder than it is."

"You said that about Kwesi's trick," Tag muttered. "And he still can't do it."

"That's because he *thinks* he can't do it. All he has to do is *think* he *can*, and he will. And I'm not gonna let up till he does. Mind over matter, see? Gramps says there's nothing you can't do if you put your mind to it."

"Did you ever think maybe sometimes your grandfather is wrong?" Tag asked so quietly I wasn't sure I heard him right.

"Huh?" I said.

But Tag didn't repeat it, and I didn't make him.

In another minute we rolled up on my driveway. "Lemonade. 7UP. Root beer. Cola. Moo juice," I started listing every drink I could think of as we made for the kitchen like a pair of camels finally hitting the oasis. "Orange juice. Grape juice. Yoo-Hoo. Kool-Aid. Yenta Juice . . . ," I paused for Tag to respond, to crack a smile—and he did. He couldn't help it. Yenta Juice came from one of Wild Willie's best routines—the one about the debonair and rotten Mr. Snide who glug-glugs his secret potion, Yenta Juice 95, and turns into the busybody

Dr. Schmeckle, who wants to help everybody so much he drives them all crazy.

"Better go easy on that stuff," said Tag.

"Yeah, it's dangerous," I agreed. "I'll stick to . . ."

"Six slimy sea serpents surreptitiously slithering in the shifting sand," came a voice from the living room. Except it was more like a *Voice*, with a capital *V*.

"Who is *that*?" asked Tag.

"We'll soon find out," I replied, detouring us past the kitchen.

The woman sitting on the sofa next to my father looked like a bird. A small bird—one of those wrens that nest inside the boxes Dad hangs around the outside of the house. They have the Voice, too, those wrens. You wouldn't believe how such a big sound can come from something so tiny.

"Now, you try it," said Ms. Wren.

"Six slimy slea slerpents serruptitiously slithering in the sifting sand," Dad managed to mangle.

"Let's try it again, shall we? Take your time for now. Enunciate each word clearly. Six slimy sea serpents surreptitiously slithering in the shifting sand."

There were beads of sweat on Dad's upper lip. He wiped them away absentmindedly. "Six slimy sea slerpents serruptitiously shivering in the shifting shand."

"What's going on?" Tag whispered.

I shrugged, and we made for the kitchen. We were downing a couple of quarts of apple juice when Mom flung open the back door and barreled in, bellowing, "Is she still here?"

"If you mean the six slimy sea serpents lady, the answer is yes," I said.

"Is that what they're up to now? Well, at least they got past the 'Rubber baby buggy bumpers' stage."

"Who is she, Mom?" I asked.

"Her name is Miss R-r-ro-mah-no," Mom said, over-enunciating. She's supposed to improve your father's diction for when he goes on TV." She looked at the quart of juice in my hand. "How many times have I told you to use a glass?" She took the container away from me.

"Who sent her? Dad's boss?"

Mom shook her head. "Who do you think?"

I thought for about three seconds. "Gramps," I said.

"You got it," said Mom, then she lifted the juice bottle to her lips and swigged the rest of it.

"*Sur-rep*-titiously. *Sur-rep*-titiously," we heard from the living room.

Tag was mouthing the word, whatever it meant, along with her. I poked him gently.

"Maybe she *will* help Dad," I said. "Gramps has been on TV a bunch of times, on interviews and stuff. He knows what he's doing."

"Yeah. He knows how to drive me crazy," Mom said.

70

"Uh, speaking of Gramps," I said casually. "Did he call or anything? Did he want to talk to me?"

"Nope," Mom replied, taking a hunk of cheese out of the fridge.

I just nodded, like it was no big deal. But out of the corner of my eye, I could see Tag giving me the fish-eye. For a moment I felt kind of bad again about not letting him in on the Wild Willie interview plan. But a promise is a promise. I told Gramps I'd keep it under my cap, and that's where it was staying.

Then Mom said, "You did get a note, though. Somebody dropped it in my mailbox."

"Yeah? Where is it?"

"Here." She handed me an envelope with unicycles all over it. I opened it up. On the piece of paper inside was one sentence: "Last chance to let me in on the carnival." It was signed "Topper."

I felt my neck get itchy and my fingers clench. Over my shoulder, Tag read it and then gave me a concerned look.

"Who's it from?" Mom asked, her mouth full of Muenster.

"Nobody," I growled, crumpling the note and pitching it into the garbage can. "Nobody at all."

CHAPTER

TEN

I was doing battle with six slimy sea serpents that kept trying to slip into my socks while my gang cheered, when the bell rang.

"End of round one," the referee sang. He looked just like Tag. "Beginning of round two."

A second later my opponent came bounding into the ring with boxing gloves the size of cinder blocks and headgear like the Mad Hatter's. It was Topper. He danced around me, jabbing and grinning. I growled and threw a punch. But before it connected, the bell rang again and the whole dream suddenly faded like a picture drawn on a steamy windshield.

I squinted at my clock. Six-thirty on a Saturday morning—no Wild Willie, no school, no reason to be up yet, and some fool was ringing my doorbell.

I got out of bed, stubbing my toe, and hobbled into the hall. Mom and Dad's door was shut as tight as my uncle Arlen's wallet. Blinking a few times to try and focus my half-closed eyes, I stumbled down the stairs and opened the front door.

If I'd been in the mood for laughing, I don't know what would have made me laugh more—the guy's hairdo, so slick his head must've been waterproof, or his outfit, a vanilla-colored sports coat, matching shorts, and knee socks. He had a big briefcase leaning against his legs and a camera slung over one shoulder. He must be a salesman, I thought, but I couldn't begin to guess what he was selling at this time of the morning in that getup.

"Hi. Nice T-shirt. Good eyebrows. Trim your toenails. Don't wear plaid," he rat-a-tat-tatted.

I sneaked a look at my T-shirt to see which one I was wearing (it was the one that said "Don't You Wish You Were Me") and asked, "Who are you?"

The guy whipped out a card and handed it over. It said "Charlton Chase. Cosmetic Engineer." I didn't know whether that meant he was a house painter or the Avon lady. Whatever he was, I figured he had the wrong place, and I told him so.

But Charlton Chase wasn't having it. "This is 34 Powers Road, isn't it? Dan Wiggins lives here, doesn't he? The TV weatherman?"

"I'm Dan Wiggins," my dad said, shuffling up behind me before I could get out another word. He was wearing his old blue bathrobe, with the frayed collar and ripped pocket, the one he refuses to throw away even though Mom bought him a new one for Christmas. His glasses were crooked and his hair was standing straight up on one side of his head, like a lawn someone had mowed only half of. I've seen him look better in the morning. I've also seen him look worse.

I handed him the guy's card. Straightening his glasses, he read it. I could tell it didn't make any more sense to him than it did to me.

"What exactly do you do, Mr. . . . uh . . . Chase?" Dad, who's as polite as Tag, asked.

"Make-overs," this Chase character answered, sounding surprised that he had to explain. "I'm here to make you over from head to toe. Some C.E.'s want to see you first at your best, but I want to see you at your worst. I want to see the raw material before I dab, drape, and adorn it to bring out the masterpiece buried inside." He took a deep breath, like he was getting ready to dive into a pool, opened his Polaroid, clicked off a startled shot of Dad's "raw material," said, "Now, if you don't mind, I'd like to check your wardrobe," and eased his way past us into the house.

While Dad tried to stop Mr. Chase from examining his closet, and Mom, awakened at last by the noise, stomped out of their room in her "Not a Morning Person" nightshirt and shrilled, "What in Helsinki's going on here?" the phone rang.

"I'll get it," I said, though nobody heard me. "Now what?" I demanded into the receiver.

"Is he there yet?" asked Gramps.

"If you mean the makeup man, yeah," I said.

"Make-*over*, Wheel. *Make-over*, as in getting your

74

father to look like the guy on TV you'll believe when he tells you it's going to pour instead of looking like the guy most likely to go out without his rain-coat."

"*You* sent this guy?" I asked, kind of surprised even though I shouldn't have been. Besides the slimy sea serpents lady, we'd also had a dance teacher to improve Dad's posture and a masseur to help him relax, all sent by Gramps. "At six-thirty on a Saturday morning?"

" 'This guy' is the best in the business. He's booked to the limit; wasn't even sure he could make it today. I'm glad he did. Dan will be glad, too, once he sees what a whiz he is. And if he isn't glad, let him tell me so himself!"

"I don't know, Gramps," I said, doubtful for once.

"*He's* behind this, isn't he? I knew it!" Mom's voice descended from the top of the stairs. "Dan, you've got to talk to that man."

"Your mom will be glad, too," Gramps chuckled, hearing her in the background. "Eventually. . . . So, how's the carnival shaping up?"

"Great, great. Mike can leg press her dad's sad-dle. Kong's thinking of learning how to use a lasso. Tag and I are working on bucking-bronco wheelies. It's great." I didn't tell him that Kwesi still knew only one trick—even though I'd showed him sev-eral from a magic book—or that Corey and Tara were still bellyaching.

"Saddles, lassos, bucking-bronco wheelies.

75

Sounds like you're putting on a wild West show."

"Well, the emcee's pretty wild, but I don't know if he's from the West." I paused, waiting for Gramps to say something like, "Oh, yes, speaking of Wild Willie . . . ," but he didn't. So I said it instead. "Speaking of Wild Willie, did you hear from him yet?"

"Not yet. But I told you, don't worry—"

"Who is that? Is that Pete?" Mom barked, tramping toward me and the phone. "I want to give him a piece of my mind. Sending somebody here at six-thirty on a Saturday morning!"

"Tell her she's too pretty to worry about losing a little beauty sleep. And keep those broncos bucking," Gramps said, and hung up.

Mom grabbed the phone out of my hand and started to let loose into the receiver for a couple of seconds until she realized it was dead. Then she slammed it down. "I'll be in the basement doing the laundry, if anyone needs me, and nobody better need me," she warned, stomping away.

I figured I wouldn't be able to fall back asleep either, so I grabbed some breakfast, then went up to my room and threw on some clothes. On my way out, I passed Mom and Dad's room. Dad was standing by the mirror, looking bewildered in the fancier of his two suits, which I think is the one he got for his honeymoon. It had lapels wide enough for a mouse to toboggan down.

"Well, I see we have our work cut out for us," said the cosmetic engineer.

Poor Dad, I thought, but then I remembered what Gramps had said about how this make-over guy was tops and how Dad would be glad when he looked all polished and suave. Gramps is right, I told myself, getting on my bike. You want to be a Big Wheel, you gotta look and act the part.

But as I rode away I couldn't help remembering Tag saying, "Did you ever think sometimes your grandfather might be wrong?" I had to hum Wild Willie's theme song to drive the thought out of my head.

CHAPTER

ELEVEN

t was too early to go over to anyone's house, even Tag's, and nothing was open yet except for a couple of breakfast places and the laundromat. Since I didn't feel like watching somebody's underwear spinning around in a dryer, I aimed for the park. But then I took a turn and ended up by the old railroad tracks instead.

It was quiet there. Real quiet. Gramps says he remembers when trains used to pass through here. But that was a long time ago. The only sounds now were bees buzzing as they darted in and out of the wildflowers that had taken over the tracks and birds chirping in the bushes and marsh beyond. Gramps says, "Nature abhors a vacuum," which means nature can't stand an empty space. This spot proved it—there wasn't a space anywhere that a weed or a reed hadn't filled. It didn't look as bad as the Old Wembley Place, though, or at least how the Old

Wembley Place had looked when I'd last seen it. Here the weeds and reeds seemed to belong and were taking back what had once been theirs.

Comparing the tracks to the Old Wembley Place made me wonder what Topper and his dad were doing to it, which made me think about Topper, which made my eyes narrow and my neck itch. It had been a couple of days since he'd sent that note: "Last chance to let me in on the carnival." His threat didn't scare me. What was he going to do? Beat me up? I was bigger than he was. Probably stronger, too. Tell people not to come to the carnival? Nobody would listen. Steal my gang? Right—as if they'd rather be with a show-off like him instead of a Big Wheel like me!

I laughed out loud. A red-winged blackbird flew up onto a branch and screeched at me. "Ah, tell it to the judge," I yelled back.

"Better pipe down, Wheel, or we'll have to run you in for disturbing the peace," Officer Birdsall said, trotting along the tracks in the opposite direction, with his partner, Officer McPhail.

He'd spooked me so much I forgot to be polite. "What are you doing here?"

"Got a report there was a suspicious-looking character lurking around. Looks like we caught him."

"Stop pulling his leg, Bob," Officer McPhail told me. "We're looking for a stolen bike. You see any?"

"No, but I hope you find it," I said, getting on my own wheels.

"Hey, what happened to the rest of your gang?" Officer Birdsall asked. "They ditch you?"

"The day they do that, you'll be the first to know about it, Officer Birdsall," I said, tipping my *Marietta Messenger* cap to him and riding away. I didn't scratch my itchy neck until I was sure he was well out of sight.

Tag was ready to go when I picked him up. We were rehearsing that day at Kong's, and I'd already told everybody else to meet us there. On the way I entertained him with the story of Charlton Chase, Cosmetic Engineer. I'd been keeping Tag and the rest of my gang posted on Dad's progress.

Tag laughed, but then he said, "I feel sorry for your dad. It's like he's not being allowed to be himself."

"Sure he is," I said. "Inside he'll be the same. It's just his outside that's gonna change."

"Maybe he doesn't want his outside to change."

"Well, it has to, if he's gonna make it on TV."

Tag shrugged, then he said, "I like your dad the way he is. He's interesting—all the stuff he knows about weather and history and the origins of words."

"My dad?" My eyebrows rose. I mean, I liked my dad, too—he was my father, after all. But interesting? I wouldn't exactly call him that. And I was surprised Tag would after having to listen politely to all of Dad's odd data for years.

We didn't get to discuss it further because just then we reached Kong's. The driveway was full of bikes. The yard was full of my gang, watching Kong and laughing.

"You can do that trick, Kwesi. You'll be great. You'll all be great. I'm great, and you're great, and Wild Willie's great. It's great to be great!" Kong boomed, strutting around. "And if you don't like that, you can lump it!"

When he saw me, he stopped. "Hi, Wheel," he said, looking a little embarrassed.

Everyone else looked kind of embarrassed, too.

"Working on a new act?" I asked, friendly.

"Yeah," Kong said. "Impressions of the Not-So-Rich-and-Somewhat-Famous."

I laughed, and so did the rest of my gang. Gramps always said, "Imitation is the sincerest form of flattery," and I believed it. Then, looking around, I asked, "Where's Tara?"

Nobody answered.

"She's okay, isn't she? She's not sick?"

"No, she's not sick," Brian answered slowly.

"So, where is she?"

He pulled his ear, something he does when he's nervous. "At Topper's," he said, at last. "He's showing her his attic. . . . But we don't need her anyway. She's a pain."

First I felt like someone had whacked me from behind with a well-packed snowball. Then my neck started to itch something fierce. I scratched it casually. It was one thing to be disturbed, but another thing to show it. "She'll have to work twice as hard tomorrow," I said with a shrug, like it was no big deal.

But inside I thought, One point to you, Topper, and you'd better believe it's the only one you're gonna score!

CHAPTER

TWELVE

Your grandfather's out on a story, Wheel," Gina Suzuki, the receptionist at Gramps's office, said, with a smile for me and Tag.

"That's okay. I didn't come to see him. I came to see you," I replied, leaning on her desk.

"Yeah? To what do I owe this honor?" She winked at Tag and leaned forward, like she really wanted to hear what I had to say.

Tag was turning all kinds of colors. Gina once told him he had the most gorgeous red hair. I thought he was going to faint then. Later he told me he thinks Gina's the prettiest woman he's ever seen. I think she's pretty, too. But I can handle it. I took out a pack of gum, offered her a stick, popped one in my own mouth, and chewed a while before I said, "There's this friend of mine I'm playing a little joke on. He'll be coming here tomorrow to meet a reporter named Charles Foster Kane. What he won't know is Charles Foster Kane is me."

"So, you want me to play along, huh?"

"Yeah. You got it." I grinned.

The phone rang. *"Marietta Messenger,"* Gina informed the caller. "I'm sorry you thought the summer solstice cake tasted like sawdust, Ms. Schermer. I'll pass that along to our food editor. Good-bye. *Marietta Messenger.* . . . That was a humorous piece, Mr. Okie. Ms. Locklin doesn't hate people who like country-and-western music. . . . Yes, I'll tell her. . . . Good-bye. *Marietta Messenger.* . . . The same to you!" She slammed down the phone and gave me a thumbs-up before it rang again.

"We're gonna use Gramps's computer for a while," I told her. Tag, who had seemed rooted to the floor, moved so fast he bumped into me.

I shook my head and gave him a little shove in the direction of Gramps's office.

He sank into Gramps's big soft "thinking" chair to recover from his brush with beauty. I slid behind the desk, moused over to the word processing program and started typing a letter that began "Dear Topper Smith."

Smith. I snorted. It was Tara who'd told me the kid's last name. No wonder he called himself Topper. His real name was probably John or Jim or something equally forgettable, and that kid did not want to be forgotten.

What he did want to do was to steal my gang. That was definitely his plan.

First he'd hooked Tara.

"It's his pool, right?" I had asked Brian when Tara hadn't shown up for the second day in a row.

"No. That isn't filled yet," Brian told me. "She says he's got this great attic with good stuff for costumes. He's letting her keep whatever she wants. Also, she thinks his floors are better."

"What does that mean, his floors are better?"

"They're made of hardwood. It's easier to tap-dance on hardwood."

Then later on, Kwesi got frustrated over his magic act again, and so did I. "Maybe Tara's got the right idea," he grumbled. "Maybe I should join her at Topper's."

"Yeah? You think you'd like his floors better, too?" I rapped out.

Kwesi didn't answer me. But the next day he was gone, and so was Corey.

"Topper's? They went to Topper's?" I couldn't believe it.

"Yeah," replied Kong. "Kwesi talked to him last night. Topper told him he knows a lot of magic tricks and he could teach him a few."

"And he's going to teach Corey to juggle so he can have his own act. You'd better talk to Corey, Wheel, or find somebody else to work with me," Mike warned.

"I'll talk to him, all right. I'll talk to all of them," I said.

So I did. I called them up and said they were letting me and the gang down. "A gang's like an airplane," I said, giving them one of Gramps's best tips. "It needs all its parts to fly right. So I'm telling you you'd better be at tomorrow's rehearsal if you want the gang to keep sailing."

"Why don't you come over to Topper's instead," said Tara. "His house is air-conditioned."

"I'm not letting anybody down," said Kwesi. "I've learned two whole tricks already, and Topper says I can learn six or seven more. And he's a lot more patient than you. When I get tired, he lets me watch cartoons on his wide-screen TV."

"You don't need me at rehearsal. I already know how to be Mike's assistant. I can do that and have my own act. Topper's going to help me," Corey said. "Plus he's got the most excellent refrigerator, with a freezer full of Dooley Pops, Marshobars, and Slush Pies—enough for our whole gang doubled!"

I was plenty vexed, as Tag put it, when he came over after I'd made those calls.

"They might come back if you . . . uh . . . went a little easier on them," Tag said.

"Huh? Don't tell me you're on that kid's side, too?"

"No way," Tag said. "It's just that you've been tough lately. Kind of like a drill sergeant."

"I have to be tough. Being soft didn't work," I said.

"Hmm," said Tag. "Well, how about if you talk to Topper?"

"*Talk* to him? How? Tell him to make nice and

leave my gang alone? Forget it. You saw that guy. You read that note. You think he'd listen?"

"I guess not."

"You *know* not," I insisted. "That guy thinks he's in the cockpit. But I'm gonna push the eject button."

"What are you going to do?" Tag had asked.

And that's when I remembered Charles Foster Kane. Gramps had used his name as an alias a few times. He said it was from an old movie about a really big wheel in the newspaper business. I figured there was no reason I couldn't borrow it this once.

So that's how we ended up in Gramps's office the next day.

"Dear Topper Smith: I have recently heard about the terrific juggling act you performed in front of Marley's Hardware store," I continued the letter. "I want to interview you for my new column in the *Marietta Messenger,* 'New Kids in Town.' Please come to the newspaper office tomorrow at ten A.M. Thank you. Sincerely, Charles Foster Kane." I looked over the letter, then I called to Tag, "Okay. What do you think?"

He got up and read the letter over my shoulder. "Suppose he can't make it tomorrow?" Tag asked when he'd finished.

"Oh, he'll make it all right. You think that kid is gonna turn down the opportunity to get his name in the paper? You can bet he'll tell Tara, Kwesi, and

Corey about it, too. He'll call them up and brag to them about it, saying not to come over tomorrow because he's gotta go be famous. Then they'll show up for our rehearsal, and Topper will look like a jerk. You just wait and see."

"Hmm," said Tag.

"That's all you can say?" I said. "Just 'hmm'?"

"I hope it works, that's all. He might figure out the scam. That jerk's pretty clever."

"He's not that clever."

"Hmm," Tag repeated.

"What is it with you? You think I can't deal with this kid? He's an annoyance, that's all. A minor annoyance. A stone stuck in my sneaker. A mosquito trying to mess up my sleep. One good swat, and he's gone," I declared, slapping my hand on the table. If I could get Tag to believe it, maybe I'd believe it, too. But the fact was Topper was beginning to feel more like a shark than a mosquito.

Tag jumped. "Okay, okay," he said. "You're right. This scheme will work." Then he murmured, "I guess."

I didn't want to waste time trying to convince him. Whoever said "actions speak louder than words" was right in my book.

So I printed up the letter on *Marietta Messenger* stationery, stuffed it neatly into an addressed envelope, and said, "Let's go. You can play lookout while I slip this into his mailbox."

"In broad daylight?" Tag's eyes widened.

"When else? If he's supposed to come here to-morrow, he's got to get the letter today."

"Maybe he's already collected his mail."

"Maybe it'll snow on the Fourth of July," I re-torted.

"It's been known to happen . . . in Australia," Tag said, deadpan.

"Right," I replied. "With a little luck maybe Top-per will move there next."

Tag snickered.

I pulled his T-shirt out of his shorts. He threw a fake punch at me, then tucked his shirt back in.

"Tracks?" I said.

"Tracks," he agreed, and we headed into the lobby.

But one look at Gina Suzuki and he had to go comb his hair. While I was waiting for him, Gramps appeared.

"Hey, just the man I want to see," he said, squeezing my shoulder.

"You've got five messages here, Pete," Gina said to him. "And one package."

"Is it ticking?" he asked.

"Ha-ha," she replied.

Gramps wiggled his eyebrows at her, then turned to me. "I tried calling you this morning, but no one answered. I've got a little piece of news concerning your favorite deejay," he said. His voice was so solemn and his mouth so tight my face hit the bot-tom of my high tops. Wild Willie must have nixed the interview, which meant I probably wouldn't win the contest. He wouldn't be our emcee. My gang would jump ship, permanently. And that shark Topper would have me for breakfast. In three seconds I'd imagined my whole world doing the old crash and crumble, and I wasn't used to such a picture.

Then, still in the same serious voice, Gramps said, "The news is July first, ten A.M., WZIP studios."

"Huh?" I said, not understanding what I wasn't expecting.

"July first, ten A.M., WZIP," Gramps repeated. "That's the where and when. The what is one interview. The who is you, me, and Wild Willie makes three."

"Hot dawg!" I threw my cap in the air.

"And boola-boola!" Gramps finished with me.

We jumped around, high- and low-fiving each other. "See, told you not to worry," Gramps declared.

And all of a sudden, I wasn't. Everything that had seemed so cloudy and gray not two minutes before was all blue skies. Wild Willie had said yes. I was going to win the contest. My gang would stick to me tighter than ticks. And Topper would be left swimming all alone in his own tank. I patted my pocket with the letter from Charles Foster Kane. Yessirree. Everything was coming up petunias.

Then a voice cut in, "You're going to interview Wild Willie?"

I looked up. Tag was standing in the doorway, looking stunned—and this time it wasn't because of Gina Suzuki. "You're going to interview Wild Willie," he repeated, "and you're not taking me?"

"Whoops," I said lamely, and I gave him a lopsided grin.

Tag didn't stay mad for long, at least not about not getting to meet Wild Willie. I told him he'd meet Wild Willie anyway at the carnival, where the Man was sure to be our emcee. Tag seemed to understand that. What he couldn't seem to get was why I hadn't told him about the interview in the first place. He said it was one thing to keep the Old Wembley Place a secret to give him a pleasant surprise. But this kind of surprise wasn't pleasant at all. In fact, it was lousy.

"But I just told you that Gramps told me not to tell anyone," I said.

"I'm not just *anyone*," Tag huffed.

"I know that. And I felt bad about not telling you. But I didn't want to tell you about something you couldn't do because I didn't want you to feel left out," I said, thinking that would do the trick.

But he still didn't want to let it go. "You didn't want me to tell anyone else," he grumbled.

"Coming through," a delivery guy said, trying to push between us up the *Marietta Messenger* building steps, where we were sitting.

I shifted to let him by. Then I admitted to Tag, "Well, okay. Yeah. I didn't."

91

But that didn't work either. "That's just great! I'm really glad to know how much you trust me, Wheel," he complained sarcastically, and I didn't know whether it was the complaining or the sarcasm that surprised me more.

"Hey, look," I answered, getting annoyed. "It's been hard enough for me to keep it a secret. I kept worrying that *I* was going to spill the beans. I didn't want to worry about *two* of us doing it."

Tag kind of humphed and didn't say anything for a while. I figured he was trying to decide whether or not to forgive me, so I tried to give him some time. But he took so long that I got impatient and said, "So, are you gonna help me play postman or not?"

He chewed his lip, and then he said, "All right. Let's go." But he didn't sound all that enthusiastic about it.

The last time I'd seen the Old Wembley Place, it was still in its sorry state. But when we pulled up to the driveway, I had to do a double take. The house looked like Charlton Chase, Cosmetic Engineer, had been at it. It was getting a real make-over.

Less than two weeks after Topper and his dad had taken it over, it already had a fresh paint job, shiny gates, and neatly trimmed bushes. The driveway was still weedy, but the place was starting to look good, and that bugged me. No wonder Kwesi, Corey, and Tara liked to hang out there and were probably hanging out right then, in Topper's amazing attic or his lovely living room or on his luscious lawn, sipping soda after soda, eating Dooley Pop after Dooley Pop, which the kid could obviously afford.

Well, I thought, I didn't have his house or his money. But I did have my smarts, and I was going to use them. I was going to pull that unicycle out from under Topper so fast he'd be pedaling air before he knew it.

"Hey, Wheel. Come on," Tag said. He was afraid we were going to get caught even though we hadn't done anything yet. I wasn't scared the way he was. Even if someone did catch us, I figured I could bluff my way out of it. But I'd upset Tag once already, so I didn't want to do it again.

"Okay," I said, opening the mailbox, a fancy thing with goofy-looking birds all over it. There was some mail inside, and I glanced through it, but it was just the usual stuff: fliers from stores and a couple of bills addressed to Mr. William Smith.

"Wheel," Tag warned.

"Okay, okay." I shoved the mail back in and took Charles Foster Kane's letter out of my pocket to add to the pile.

"Wheel! Someone's coming down the driveway," Tag hissed. "I think it's Topper's father."

"Doesn't that guy have a job?" I growled, tossing my envelope into the box, shutting it, and hopping on my bike.

By the time Mr. William Smith hit the end of the drive, Tag and I had left nothing but dust—and one letter—behind.

CHAPTER

THIRTEEN

The wrens were singing, the roses were blooming, Wild Willie was outdoing himself on the radio, and I was ha-ha-ing about how in a few hours Topper would be heading over to the *Marietta Messenger* to be creased, fleeced, and released. It was a scam Wild Willie would appreciate, I thought. Maybe I'd get to tell him about it sometime.

"It was so beautiful when I woke up this morning," the Man was saying. "The breeze from my Superblast Air Infiltrator was nice and fresh, and the sunlight was pouring in from my Ultra-Ray Tan-o-Beam. It was shining right on the keyboard of my computer. I got out of bed and went to take a look.

"Hmm, what's this? A new button! I had to bend down to read it. It said Press Me. Press Me? Forget it. I'm not stupid, right? Why would I press a button that said Press Me? Right? Right? So, what did I do? Huh? What do you think I did?"

"You pressed the button," I said to the radio as I slipped on a clean T-shirt.

"I pressed the button," said Wild Willie.

I laughed.

"And all of a sudden," he continued, "I was inside that computer. Wandering around the bits and bytes. Numbers flashing by my head. I tell you, it was scary. And then I saw another guy who looked sort of like me and sort of not, and I said, 'Who are you?'

" 'I'm your memory, man,' he answered.

" 'Yeah? Then tell me what happened at my birthday party when I was three.'

" 'You threw up on the ice cream.'

" 'Right! And when I was four?'

" 'You threw up on the cake.'

" 'And when I was fourteen?'

" 'You threw the cake out the window, and it landed on Mr. McVie, your high school principal, who happened to be passing by. He swore you'd never graduate, and he was right!'

" 'You *are* my memory!' I exclaimed. 'So how do I get out of here?'

" 'I don't remember.' "

I laughed harder and tugged on my jeans. I bet Tag and the rest of my gang were listening to this one and hee-hawing, too.

Wild Willie went on, " 'So, stop with the jokes,

and tell me the truth. How *do* I get out of here?'

" 'Ask the computer tutor,' said my memory. He pointed to a corner. Sitting in it was a chipmunk singing 'If I only had a brain.'

" 'How do I get out of here?' I asked him.

" 'Simple,' he replied. 'Follow the Yellow Flick Road.' He waved his paws and a sign appeared. Enter, it said. I stepped through it and onto a magic yellow light that flickered up and down, around and around, until there I was, back in my room, in my bed, with the fresh breeze blowing from my Superblast Air Infiltrator and the sunlight pouring in from my Ultra-Ray Tan-o-Beam. It was shining right on the keyboard of my computer. I got out of bed and went to take a look. And wouldn't you know it, there was a new button. What do you think it said?"

"Press Me," I said.

"Nope," Wild Willie replied. "It said . . ." He paused. Then, in a froggy bellow, he yelled, "Sucker!"

I roared, my shoulders shaking with admiration as well as laughter. Nobody could top Wild Willie. Nobody. Nobody could top me either, I told myself, thinking once again of that kid. "Sucker!" I cackled, wishing that instead of just picturing it in my head I could somehow see his face when he realizes he's being bamboozled. But that would be pushing things too far.

Or would it, I wondered, as I double-stepped it

down to breakfast. A new and brilliant Big Wheel idea began to tickle my brain.

"I should be back by seven, but you never know with audits," Mom told me. She's an accountant. She shuffles numbers all day long, which is just about all I can tell you about her job. "If it looks like it's going on a lot longer, I'll call you."

"They're thinking of testing Reich's cloudbuster again next week. I wish I could be there," Dad said wistfully, his nose buried in one of his meteorological magazines. He was all dressed up in a light gray suit, a paisley vest, and a red tie. His hair was blow-dried and moussed, and he had on his new glasses, with the thicker black frames. ("More professorial," Charlton Chase had said.)

"Isn't he a brand-new man?" the cosmetic engineer had said when he showed off Dad to us the night before, like he was unveiling the latest model luxury car.

"I hope not," Mom had replied. "I liked the old one." But even she had to admit he looked good.

Later, while Dad was downstairs polishing his weather vanes, Mom told me she was feeling confused about the whole TV business. "On the one hand, I want your father to do well because I always want him to do well at whatever he does. On the other hand, if he does do well, your grandfather's going to be impossible with his 'Didn't-I-tell-yous?' and his 'I-told-you-sos.' "

"So you want Dad to do well and you also want him to fail," I said.

"I want *Dad* to do well and *Gramps* to fail," Mom blurted. She clapped her hand over her mouth. "That was a terrible thing to say."

"How come you hate Gramps so much?" I asked.

Mom sighed. "I don't hate him. Not at all. In fact, there's a lot about him I like—his energy, his generosity, his guts. It's just that he always thinks he's got all the answers."

"But he does have all the answers," I said.

"*Nobody* has all the answers," Mom replied fiercely. "*Nobody*. Not me. Not you. And certainly not *Gramps*."

"Have you been talking to Tag lately?" I asked suspiciously.

"Not more than usual," Mom answered. "Why?"

"Nothing." I shrugged.

Then I spent a little time thinking about what she'd said, and I decided she and Tag were wrong. Gramps *did* know everything. I'd doubted him about Charlton Chase, but Gramps had said he was the best in the biz, and he sure had proved it with Dad.

"The guys at the weather station are going to be impressed with how you look today," I told my father, as I gobbled a mouthful of Wheaties. I'd set things in motion with Topper and with my gang, and I was in a hurry to watch them roll.

"He's not going to work today," Mom said, sounding annoyed. "Gramps is taking him to be photographed and to meet an agent, which he needs like a hole in the head." She turned to Dad. "I don't understand why you can't tell him to leave you alone, Dan."

Dad put down his magazine and looked at Mom. "Ellen, are you going to get on my case, too?" he said quietly. I couldn't tell if he was angry, sad, or just tired. But I did know it was a tone he hadn't used before. I studied him with interest.

Mom picked up his hand and kissed it.

Then Tag knocked on the door.

"Gotta go," I said, jumping up.

"What's the rush? You didn't even finish your breakfast yet," Mom said.

I picked up the bowl and downed the rest of my Wheaties in three gulps. "Finished," I said, and raced out of the room.

They were all there at Brian's house, just the way I thought they'd be—Tara, Kwesi, and Corey, with the rest of my gang.

"Well, look who's here," I said, like I was really surprised to see them. "You get tired of Topper's refrigerator, or was it his hardwood floors?"

"Topper's busy today," Kwesi explained. "He's going to be interviewed for your grandfather's newspaper."

"Yeah?" said Brian.

"Fancy that," said Kong in his fake British accent. But he seemed intrigued.

Even Mike looked impressed.

"Topper's going to be famous." Tara hugged herself like Topper's becoming famous would make her famous, too.

"Right. I'll bet," I said, like I didn't believe it. Out of the corner of my eye I could see Tag picking lint off his shirt. Tag can keep a straight face as long as he doesn't have to look at you.

"It's true," said Corey. "He got this letter from this reporter, Charles Foster Crain."

"Kane," Tag blurted.

"Yeah, that's right. Kane. How'd you know?"

Everybody looked at Tag, except for me. I didn't want to kill the guy with the daggers that were coming out of my eyes.

"Uh . . . uh . . . ," he stammered. Then suddenly, he pulled himself together, and, cool as a Sno-Kone, he said, "Because he's famous, that's why. His column wins awards. Isn't that true, Wheel?"

I had to hand it to him. It was an amazing recovery, especially for Tag, who's never been good at stretching the truth. It was a neat stretch, too, considering that most of my gang didn't read the *Marietta Messenger,* and the ones that did wouldn't notice the bylines. It reminded me of why I trusted him in the first place.

My response was as smooth as a .400 hitter's swing. "Yeah, he is famous," I said. "And if he's going to interview that Topper kid, I'm going to take up ballet dancing this week."

"Ms. Goldring would like that," said Tara. "She's

100

always looking for more boys to join her class."

I ignored her. So did Kwesi and Corey. "But it is true," said Kwesi. "We saw the letter," Corey added.

"I'm sure you did," I replied. "But what makes you so sure that Mr. Charles Foster Kane wrote it?"

"If he didn't, who did?" asked Corey.

"Maybe the kid himself."

Kwesi, Corey, and Tara protested that that couldn't be. But I could hear doubt creeping into their voices.

And then the idea that had been tickling my brain became a real itch, and I decided to scratch it. "What time is the kid's interview supposed to be?" I asked.

"Ten o'clock," Kwesi answered.

I made a big show of looking at my watch. "Nine-thirty. We've got plenty of time."

"Plenty of time for what?" asked Corey.

"For a little post-interview welcoming party at the *Messenger*."

"What?" Tag exclaimed, staring at me in disbelief.

"We're going to meet Topper after his interview?" Kwesi asked.

"No," Tag mouthed, nixing the idea with his hands.

"Yeah," I declared. "And five will get you ten, either the kid won't be there, the interviewer won't be there, or neither of them will be. Right, Tag?" I clapped him on the back.

He swallowed his spit the wrong way and started

choking. "Uh . . . right," he finally got out, shaking his head.

I gave him a confident "Don't Worry I Know What I'm Doing" smile, and we were off.

We pulled up to the *Messenger* building at 10:06. Forty-five minutes later, there was still no sign of the kid. The sun had stopped shining. Heavy thunderheads were starting to roll in. My gang was fidgeting. Tag was keeping to himself, making weird shapes out of a couple of paper cups he'd found.

Then, at last, I said, "See, what did I tell you? The kid didn't show." I was lying, of course. I knew in my gut that Topper was inside on the second floor, sitting in a green chair opposite Gina Suzuki's desk, waiting for Charles Foster Kane to appear. I thought it was a great scam, sneaky and classy, to pretend that I believed it was the kid who was pulling the hoax. And when he would finally emerge, looking like a fool, if my gang suspected me of being the joker, so what? So good, even. They'd know once and for all who was the real general—who'd won the war.

"Maybe he's still inside," Corey said.

"Let's go in and find out," said Tara.

"Yeah, let's," agreed Kwesi and Brian.

"Sure," I said. I was tired of waiting for my victory. "Why not?"

But before I took a single step, the front door swung open and out came Topper, juggling a jar of mayonnaise, a head of lettuce, a loaf of bread, a can of tuna, and a basket. With him was a woman in a fancy purple suit, chuckling in appreciation and taking notes. I recognized her. She was Mary Lock-lin, the features editor for the paper. But she didn't seem to notice me at all. "Thanks, Topper," she said. "This will be a great story. Look for it next week."

Topper tossed the bread, the lettuce, the tuna, and the mayonnaise into the basket and handed it to her. "Lunch," he said.

"My favorite!" She laughed. "You're terrific. I'm glad you asked if I wanted to interview you. You can tell 'Charles Foster Kane,' if he ever shows up, the joke's on him. . . . Bye, Topper. Bye, kids." She hurried down the steps and into her car.

Topper waved to her. Then he turned to us. He was still on the top step, while my gang and I were on the bottom.

"Hi, Topper," Tara cooed.

"Hi, Tara . . . ," he replied, "Kwesi . . . Corey . . . Brian . . . Mike . . . Kong . . . Tag . . . and, of course, Mr. Big Wheel." He grinned down at me. "What brings you here? Did you come to visit your grandfather? I don't think he's in. Ms. Suzuki kept taking messages for him."

"We didn't come to see Wheel's grandpa," Tara answered. "We came to see you. Wheel didn't believe you were really going to get interviewed."

"No? I wonder why." He grinned at me again. "Don't you, Tag?" Topper shot his eyes at him and then back to me. It drove me nuts. I wanted to bop him.

Tag dropped a paper cup and muttered something no one could catch.

"What did you say?" Topper asked.

"I said 'knight to king two—check.' It's a chess move," he explained reluctantly.

"A winning one?" asked Topper.

I flashed Tag a look. He dropped the other cup and didn't answer.

"Topper!" someone called.

We all turned our heads. The kid's father had pulled up to the curb in a shiny minivan. "Finished?" he asked.

"Yes," Topper said. "It's going to rain. Anyone else need a ride?"

Kwesi, Corey, and Tara raced for the car and piled their bikes inside. Brian looked at me, then up at the sky, then down at his shoes and back at me. "Wheel, I've got brand-new high tops," he said.

"So?" I demanded.

"Come on, Wheel," Brian begged, looking at the sky again.

"Come on what?" I snapped.

Brian sighed. "Sorry," he said and wheeled his bike hurriedly to Topper's Dad's van.

We—Mike, Kong, Tag, and I—watched them drive away in silence. Then I ordered, "Let's go rehearse now."

"Maybe we ought to wait until the rain passes," Mike suggested.

"It's not going to rain," I said.

"Did your dad give you that forecast?" Kong joshed.

"I think Mike's right, Wheel," Tag said quietly. "We should wait until the storm passes."

He was looking at me with a funny expression on his face. I thought he might be angry at me for wasting his time with a plan that had failed as miserably as our school's "No Throwing Food in the Lunchroom" rule. It took me a moment to realize what he was feeling. It was pity. My good buddy Tag was feeling sorry for me. As far back as I could remember, nobody had ever felt sorry for me—and as sure as my name's Wheel Wiggins, I didn't want anybody feeling that way now, especially not Tag McGill.

"I said it's not going to rain," I growled, wiping that pitiful look right off Tag's face.

We were only halfway home when it started to pour.

C H A P T E R

F O U R T E E N

Just when you think
That things really stink
And you're hollering for mercy
They can always get worse, see?

That's what the yellowing scrap of paper stuck in Mom's mirror said.

I'll tell you, it's bad news when your life resembles a lousy poem.

All the carnival posters were printed. The food and game booths were coming along great. Gramps had advertised the big event in his paper. Thanks to the interview, which was coming up fast, Wild Willie was sure to be our mystery guest emcee. Everyone, but everyone, was looking forward to the carnival, or, as Gramps called it, the "Show of Shows."

I should have been on top of the world. Instead

I was down in the dumps, worrying day and night that the Show of Shows was going to be the Woe of Woes.

Brian was gone, along with Kwesi, Corey, and Tara, all of them busy sliding down Topper's super-duper banisters, laughing at cartoons on his wide-screen TV, or watching his pool get filled.

"That's it. They're dusted," I declared.

"Dusted?" said Tag.

"Dusted. Fired. Axed. They can't make it to rehearsals, they can't be in the carnival."

"But their names are on the poster. And we hardly have enough acts as it is."

"So what?" I said, like it was no big deal. But it was, and I was going to have to come up with something, although I didn't know what. For a while I thought about recruiting some of the other kids I knew. But I chucked the idea. First of all, I needed them for the booths and the audience. Second, and worse, I kept imagining that if I let them join my gang, that sneak thief Topper would steal them, too.

As for the rest of my gang—what was left of it— they were droopy and slow. The thunderstorm had kicked off days of rain and high humidity, which wouldn't let us rehearse outdoors. Kong, who never lost his temper, snapped at me when I tried to improve his gorilla wrestling technique. Mike said she didn't have the energy to lift a Barbie doll, let alone a barbell. Tag didn't say much one way or the other.

I was beginning to wonder if maybe it wasn't just Topper or the weather. What had happened to my Big Wheel touch? I didn't know how to get it back because I couldn't see how I'd lost it in the first place. So, like the poem said, things really did stink. And yeah, ditto, they were about to get worse.

The day the spit hit the can was a ten on the sunburn index. I was so glad to see Old Sol that I didn't care about the heat. I figured my gang would feel the same way. We'd be able to make up for lost time, and I'd decided what to do to make up for lost people. It was simple. We'd double up on the acts. "You want me to lift weights *and tap-dance*?" Mike stared at me.

"It's on the poster—Tara the Tap-Dancing Wonder. Tara's out. You've got to be her. Ms. Ridley from Dancerama is going to help you. I called her last night. Kong, you're going to do Kwesi's bit. Mr. LoVecchio will teach you."

"Loggerhead LoVecchio?" Kong exclaimed, imitating the teacher's turtlelike expression. "He knows magic?"

"Yeah. He showed us some tricks a couple of years ago, remember?"

"The biggest trick was that nobody passed out from his breath when he leaned over us in class," Mike retorted.

One of Gramps's favorite tips came into my head. "Look, desperate times require desperate measures," I said.

"Nothing could be that desperate, my man," said Kong.

"Ms. Ridley and Mr. LoVecchio will be over here around twelve-thirty."

Kong and Mike gave each other a strange look, then immediately glanced down at their watches.

"Don't worry," I said. "You've got time before then to work on your other acts. Tag, you'll be Mike's assistant, let her lift you and stuff."

He shook his head. "I can't," he said.

"What do you mean, you can't? There's nothing to it."

"I can't," he repeated, stubbornly.

I didn't know why he was protesting. "What, are you all of a sudden scared of heights?" I said, trying to make a joke of it.

"No. . . . I'm ticklish," he finally revealed, unhappily. "Very ticklish."

I'd forgotten about that little problem of Tag's. "So? Mike won't tickle you," I responded.

But Mike did. First it was intentional, and Tag kicked and yelled and slapped at her. I told her to cut it out, and she did. But it didn't help. Just the touch of her fingers or toes on his waist, and Tag began kicking and yelling and slapping once more. I had to make Kong Mike's assistant, and soon they began to complain.

"We can't do *everything* in this show, Wheel," Kong said seriously, looking at his watch again.

"Kong's right. We can't," agreed Mike, looking at hers.

109

"Let me see that lift again," I replied. They groaned. Tag frowned. The sun got hotter. We were all sweating like crazy, but I hardly noticed.

Then, when it was almost noon, Mike said, "We need a break, Wheel."

"Yeah, let's go inside and get something to drink," Kong backed her up. They gave each other that funny look again.

"Okay. But not a long one. Remember, Loggerhead and Ms. Ridley will be here soon."

We went into my kitchen. I got out some sodas. I thought Mike and Kong would gulp theirs down the way Tag and I were doing. But they were both kind of sipping slowly and looking at the clock.

"How's your dad doing?" Mike made conversation. "Is he excited about being on TV?"

"Hel-lo, Sun!" Kong yelled, mimicking this obnoxious weatherman from a rival TV station.

"He's doing good. He's got a new look and a new agent. Gramps says she's a real go-getter."

"That's great," said Mike. She and Kong glanced at the clock again.

"Yeah," I said. "It *is* time to get back to work." I stood up and looked at Tag. He was tying some fancy knot in a piece of twine someone had left on the table. It took him a few seconds to notice me; then he rose, too.

"Uh, we didn't finish our drinks yet," said Kong, not budging.

"Take 'em outside with you," I said.

"Got any cookies to go with these?" Mike asked.

110

"Sure." I grabbed a package from the cabinet. "We can take these along, too. Come on. We don't have any time to waste."

Mike and Kong got up, moving like two dinosaurs in a tar pit. Then the phone rang, and they both jumped about a foot. I squinted at them while I picked up the receiver.

"Hello, Wiggins Wigwam. Wheel the Wise speaking."

There was a slight chuckle, and then a voice that was all too familiar, even though I'd only heard it a few times before, said, "So, Big Chief Wheel, are you ready for a truce?"

It was the kid. I had to hand it to him—he rattled me. "Why are you c-calling me?" I stammered.

"To invite you for a swim, along with Mike and Kong and Tag, too, if you'll let him. It's a hot day. You need to cool off."

I was steamed all right, and it cleared my head. "What you're selling, I'm not buying," I rapped out and slammed down the phone.

"Who was that?" asked Tag.

I stared back at Mike and Kong. "Ask them. They know."

Kong looked away. Mike said, "He called me and Kong last night and said that his pool's full and invited us over today. I told him he had to ask you, too—like, you know, a personal invitation. Come on, Wheel. We can't do this carnival without the rest of the gang, and we can't get the rest of the gang without Topper."

111

For a moment, I didn't say anything. I just glared at her, my eyes burning like a bonfire. Then I said, "And you called Corey a wimp? Who's wimping out now? Well, go on then. Get out of here, you and Kong. Go have a nice little swim at that show-off's place. And don't bother to come back!"

"Oh, come on, Wheel—" Kong began.

But Mike was mad, too. "I'm a *wimp*? Well, you're a bossy, bullheaded *know-it-all*! You drove Kwesi, Kong, and Brian away, and now you've just lost me." She turned, flung herself on her bike, and rode away.

Kong shook his head at me. "Sorry, Wheel. But she's right this time," he said, and he left, too.

"Wimps!" I called after them. Then I turned to Tag. "Get on your bike," I said. "We'll work on our act."

Tag just stood there. "I don't think that's a good idea right now," he said quietly.

"I think it's an *excellent* idea. We'll work on the Vault of Death."

Tag still didn't move. "Look, I think we ought to talk, Wheel. . . ."

"We jump off this ramp," I said, setting up the course, "and fly over two boxes, down and up another ramp, across these two narrow beams, and then, zoom, right over these flaming barbecue grill things, what are they called?"

"Hibachis," Tag couldn't resist answering. "But I mean it, Wheel. I don't want to—"

". . . okay, okay, maybe we won't light them. I know, we'll stack them. We'll jump over a stack of hibachis, followed by the kiddie pool, then right onto this red carpet. Okay, let's go. Get on your bike."

"*Listen* to me," Tag said so sharply I had to shut up. "This is crazy! I'm your best friend and you know it. But Mike is *right*. We can't do this without the rest of the gang. So, maybe you ought to reconsider how you've been pushing us. You never used to push so hard, Wheel. And maybe it wouldn't be bad to let Topper be in the show after all."

"You, too?" I said. "You think I should holler uncle? I should let that creep win? I'd die first. Now, get on that bike!"

"Well, I wouldn't rather die. Or get messed up. Or mess up my bike."

"Stop whining. You're always whining. Nothing's going to happen to you or your precious Lorenzutti. So, come on—unless you want out, too."

Tag's face got hurt and angry and sad and defiant and all kinds of things at once. I knew somewhere inside I'd gone too far, but I was too hurt and angry and sad and defiant myself to stop.

We got on our bikes. I gritted my teeth. I counted, "One . . . two . . . three!"

Off we went, over the ramp, over the boxes, off the second ramp, across the beams. We were flying, really flying until we got to the hibachis. The stack

113

wasn't high, but it was narrow. Somehow, Tag's bike had gotten too close to mine, and we collided. I landed in the kiddie pool, Tag in the grass.

"Are you okay?" I asked, shaking myself off and hobbling over to him. He didn't answer.

"I said are you all right?" My voice was quivering a little. I wasn't angry anymore, just scared. I didn't want Tag hurt for anything in the world.

Tag still didn't say a word. He just sat there, staring at his bike.

I stared at it, too, and gulped. The forks were twisted, the seat was split, and the front wheel was bent. "Oh man. How'd that happen?" I said. "That shouldn't have happened. No way."

Slowly, Tag stood up, lifting the bike with him. "Well, it *did* happen, didn't it?" He looked at me, his eyes dark and hard as the coals in those little grills.

"I don't know what went wrong. You must've braked or something, Tag."

His eyes got even darker and harder. "My name is Taggart," he hissed. "*Taggart*, not *Tag-along*." Grabbing hold of the wrecked bike, he spun around and dragged it furiously out of my yard and up the street.

As I watched him go, I wanted to call him back and apologize. Instead, I yelled, "Great! Go ahead. Go to Mr. Rich Boy, with the rest of them. I don't need you. I don't need *any* of you!"

If Tag heard me, he didn't turn around. I did, though. And there were Ms. Ridley and Mr.

LoVecchio, standing behind me and looking confused.

"Rehearsal's canceled," I said, getting on my bike and riding in the opposite direction.

And there you have it—the complete, the total story of what drove me to dump fifteen pounds of very old, very smelly, very dead fish into Topper Smith's pool.

C H A P T E R

F I F T E E N

I've never been big on sleeping. It seems like a waste of time when you could be doing something more exciting. But this morning I feel like I could've used a couple more z's last night. I only got maybe an hour's worth, and it wasn't a great hour.

I had this dream that my gang was at a party at Topper's, laughing, eating Dooley Pops and having a good time. I kept trying to join in, but they wouldn't let me. "Know-it-all!" sneered Mike, before she turned her back on me. "No patience," Kwesi shook his head and walked away. The worst was Tag. He totally ignored me.

"Hey, good buddy, old pal," I said, dancing around, trying to get his attention. Finally he turned, looked me straight in the eye, and said, "Tyrant."

"No, no, no. You got me all wrong!" I said. But

he ignored me again. "You got me all wrong!" I cried so loudly that I woke myself up. I didn't even try to go back to sleep after that.

"Why does it smell like fish in here?" Mom sniffs, coming into my room now while I'm checking out my bow tie in the mirror. Gramps isn't picking me up for a couple of hours yet. But I'm already getting ready. Heck, nobody'll ever accuse me of not trying to look my best for Wild Willie.

"I don't smell anything," I lie. "Eau de Fish" is on the clothes I wore for my early morning mission, and these same clothes are hiding under my bed so I can wash them when Mom's not around.

"Last time I smelled things that weren't there, I was pregnant with you." She looks nervous.

"Gee, do you think you're going to have another bundle of joy?" I ask innocently.

"I sure hope not. One's been quite enough," she says sarcastically, but she gives me a warm hug.

Her hug does something funny to me. Suddenly I'm five years old again, and I want to blubber how weird, how bad it feels not to have Tag and the rest of my gang around. It comes on so fast and strong, this feeling, it's like somebody shoved me and I'm wobbling and windmilling to keep my balance.

Then Mom says, "Big day, huh?" and I'm okay again. I tell myself what I told myself when I woke up—that dreams are just dreams. That today's my lucky day. In a few hours I'm going to be face-to-face with Wild Willie. He's going to say yes to being emcee. And my gang is going to ditch Topper and

117

his fishy pool and come crawling back to me. I'll be big about it, too, and let them. Everything will work out. It has to.

"Yeah," I say to Mom, who knows about the interview because Gramps told her. "Big day."

"For your dad, too."

"Yeah. His premiere. Isn't it great?"

But she looks dubious. Then she goes off to work.

I flick on the radio to listen to the Man himself.

By the time Gramps comes to pick me up, Wild Willie's show is almost over and I've changed my clothes five times.

Gramps checks out my Hawaiian shirt and white sports coat. "Very *now*," he says, like Charlton Chase. He himself is wearing a pink-and-gray-striped jacket that reminds me of bubble gum.

I play along, asking, "It's not too *caj*?" which is Charltonese for "casual."

"No, not at all. It's that perfect blend of *caj* and classy," Gramps replies.

We both laugh and get into his car. The first thing I notice is that he's got a new cellular phone, and it's ringing.

He answers it. "Yes. Sure. . . . Right. . . . I know they've hired this Crabbe character. But Dan's got seniority. He's the best meteorologist they've got, and he's going to be the best TV forecaster. Tell them that if they don't want him to walk, they'd better put Crabbe on ice. Tell 'em to offer him a nice breach of contract bonus. Got it?" He hangs up.

"What was that all about?" I ask.

118

"That was your dad's agent. She's negotiating a long-term TV deal for him, but she's hit a snag— the new forecaster they've hired. I told her to work it out."

"Dad's decided he wants a long-term TV deal?" I say, amazed.

"He will when he finds out about it," Gramps replies.

Now I'm more than amazed. I'm alarmed. It's one thing to help Dad's career, but another to choose a new career for Dad without even telling him. The stuff Mom and Tag said about Gramps comes floating into my head again.

"Look, you know your dad. Sometimes he needs an extra push. Your friend Tag's a bit like that, too, isn't he?"

"Yes," I would've said just two weeks, two days ago. But now, with the image of Tag's hurt face still in my head, I'm suddenly not so sure.

I decide maybe it's time for a little man-to-man talk. "Actually, Gramps, I might have . . . um . . . pushed Tag a little too far. He's kind of ticked off at me. And the rest of my gang, some of them are ticked, too. They've stopped coming to rehearsal."

"Did you call them up and explain that when the going gets tough, the tough get going, and no pain, no gain? Did you appeal to their loyalty, tell 'em a gang's like an airplane?"

"Yeah. It didn't work. See, there's this other kid. This show-off. He's burned because I wouldn't let him in the show, and he's been doing the sneak thief number, stealing my gang."

"A sneak thief, huh? Well, with a sneak thief you can either arrest him or take away his tools."

"Or his pool," I mutter.

"Huh?" says Gramps.

"His tools," I say louder and pause. "But I still don't know about Tag. . . ."

"Don't worry about him. He'll come back. They'll all come back, especially with Wild Willie in the bag," Gramps advises.

"Yeah. Yeah, that's just what I told myself," I say.

He pats my knee and I pat his and we grin. But I'm not feeling so convinced.

We get on to other things then, namely, how I should approach Wild Willie about being emcee. I try out stuff like "It's a pleasure to meet you, Wild Willie. I've got a little favor to ask you . . ." and "So, Wild Willie, my man, I, Wheel Wiggins, want to do you a favor. You've got a lot of fans, but I can get you more. Let me tell you what you have to do" and so on. And Gramps helps. We joke around some, get serious some, and the shadow of doubt about Gramps being wrong drifts to the back of my mind.

Then we're there—at WZIP headquarters. My mouth feels like sunrise on the Sahara. My heart's taking off like a pigeon at a cat show.

"Relax," Gramps says, as I trip out of the car and practically fall on my face. "He's just another guy.

He's not any better than you or I. Even a king has to go to the toilet."

"Let's not talk about toilets," I say, shifting uncomfortably.

Through the parking lot we go, into the building, up in the elevator, past the receptionist, into the waiting room, where the *Marietta Messenger* photographer meets us. Then hello to the secretary, who takes us into the Man's office. "He'll be right with you," she says.

"Carnival, carnival, carnival. Emcee, emcee, emcee," I mutter like a prayer, while Gramps and the photographer kid around about cameras.

Finally, the door opens. I take a deep breath and smile, smile, smile, thanking my dentist for teaching me the right way to brush my teeth.

Wild Willie backs into the room, waving goodbye to someone. His farewell is about as long as a one-act play. I'm still smiling and smiling and thinking "Carnival, carnival/emcee, emcee" for all I'm worth.

Then the Man turns. "Hi," he says to Gramps and the photographer. He looks at me. "Well, hello. What a surprise!"

Surprise isn't the word for it. Even shock is too mild. A mistake. It must be a mistake, I think. I wish. Because there, standing in front of me, with his ordinary face and his ordinary height and his kind of familiar something that I realize is nothing other than his famous voice, is Topper's father, Mr. William Smith, also known as Wild Willie.

Do I really have to tell what happened?
Wild Willie was nice and cheerful. Too nice and cheerful. It didn't take me long to realize he hadn't checked out his swimming pool yet. A man with a swimming pool full of dead fish would not have been in that good a mood.

"You two know each other?" Gramps inquired, after Wild Willie asked why I wasn't hanging out at his place the way my pals were, and I mumbled something about being too busy.

"Yes," Wild Willie answered Gramps. "We met at my new house."

"You live in Marietta?"

"Uh-huh. 53 Beech Tree Road."

"The Old Wembley Place?" Even in the state I was in, I could see Gramps quivering with the excitement of a big scoop. Wild Willie, top deejay, a resident of our own hometown.

"I guess that's what they call it." Wild Willie smiled at me and then apologized for not having revealed his identity when we first met. "But as you can guess," he said, "I get hounded by a lot of fans always wanting me to do something for them."

Gramps waited for me to say something, and when I didn't, he said, "Speaking of wanting you to do something, Wheel's got this lollapalooza of a carnival planned."

He didn't have to go on much further because that's when Wild Willie explained that (a) he couldn't be emcee because of his own Fourth of July bash and (b) he couldn't pick me as the contest winner either because "it would be a conflict of interest to pick one of my son's friends."

"I'm not his friend," I muttered, and Wild Willie gave me a puzzled look.

There was nothing else to say after that, and I didn't say it. I just sat there in miserable silence through the whole rest of the interview with my world burning to bits around me.

The emcee and contest business were bad enough, but what I kept thinking over and over was that I'd messed up Wild Willie's pool, which was worse than toilet papering the White House.

I was so sunk in agony, Gramps had to tap me to let me know that the interview was finally over and that we were about to leave. Then I jerked to my feet like a puppet come to life.

Wild Willie smiled at me. "Good to see you again,

Wheel. Come on over for a swim sometime soon."

I think I groaned as I bolted for the door.

On the ride home, Gramps burbled on and on about how great the interview had gone and how terrific a scoop he'd just gotten. I didn't say a word, which he didn't seem to notice for a long time.

Then, when he said, "Nice guy, Wild Willie," and I still didn't respond, he patted my knee. "Look, it's too bad about the contest and the carnival. But what a great coincidence. You can sure use that to your advantage some other time. And I'll tell you what—*I'll* be your emcee. I'm not entirely unknown in this town, you know," he said, with false modesty. "Well, aren't you going to say *anything*?"

"No," I said.

For once, Gramps didn't press me. When we pulled up to my house, he looked at the clock in his car. "Good thing we're home. Your dad will be making his debut in twenty minutes."

I sighed. Well, at least there'll still be two Big Wheels in town, I thought, and went up to my room.

Which is where I am right now, lying on my bed, knowing I should be thinking up some great idea to save the carnival and my reputation. But nothing comes into my head. Nothing at all.

Then Mom calls, "Wheel? You up there?"

"Of course he's up there. I just told you he was," I hear Gramps tell her.

I also hear Mom ignore him. "Hurry and come on down. Your dad's about to be on TV."

I get up kind of stiffly. Not only does my leg still hurt from when I fell by Wild Willie's pool, but the rest of me feels battered, too. Slowly, I head downstairs.

Mom, who's come home from work just for this occasion, and Gramps are jostling for the best spot in front of the TV.

"We should have gone to the studio, seen him live," says Gramps.

"He told you, Pete. He didn't want an audience," Mom replies.

"Since when does Dan know what he wants?"

"Ooh. You know you drive me crazy when you say things like that!"

I slip into the easy chair and stare at the TV, where the sportscaster is finishing his report. The thought comes into my head that this is it, my last chance. Suddenly I'm excited and nervous. I told everyone but everyone about Dad's debut, and they'll all be watching. He's got to do well, not only for himself, but for me, too. "Come on, Dad. You can do it," I whisper.

"An exciting game, eh, Roger?" Symie Jefferson, the anchorwoman, says.

"Yes. A real squeaker," the sportscaster agrees.

They both look like they aren't even working, just having a friendly chat.

Then the anchorman, Ray Barbella, says, "Speaking of exciting, we have a brand-new weatherman this week—Dan Wiggins."

Mom grips the arm of the sofa. Gramps leans so far forward in his seat, his chest practically touches his knees. I tap my heels on the floor and drum my hands on my thighs.

"Hi, Dan," Symie Jefferson greets him.

The camera moves to Dad. He looks good in his suit and vest, which gives me a feeling of confidence. Then he opens his mouth. "Hi, Ray. Hi, Slimy," he says, in a voice that sounds like it belongs to an android.

"Oh no," says Mom.

I groan.

"*Sy*mie. *Sy*mie," says Gramps, as if Dad could hear him.

Dad doesn't seem to notice his mistake, and he goes on in the same robotic voice. "Now, here's today's weather joke." He takes a long pause.

"That was my idea," Gramps says proudly.

"Yeah? Who's writing the jokes?" asks Mom.

"Dan is."

Mom and I look at each other hopelessly. We know Dad's jokes. They're indecipherable to anyone who isn't a meteorologist.

This one turns out to be no exception. "Why didn't the man believe the radiosonde?" he says. I wince. I know he's talking about a weather balloon, but nobody else would. Then without even a pause, Dad goes right into the punch line, "Because it was full of hot air. Ha-ha."

This time it's Mom who groans. I'm too mortified to let out a sound.

Dad goes into today's forecast, with the temperature, humidity, and wind velocity, which he does okay, except that he still sounds like Computer Man. Then he shifts to the air masses and fronts, turning to the map to illustrate. But it's not the correct map. Some bozo's got the five-day forecast up there, and Dad stops dead, as if he short-circuited, then he panics. "That's not it. That's not the weather map. Where's the weather map?"

The same bozo flicks a switch and still doesn't get it right. Now he's got a picture of some English duchess in a bathing suit, and I'm wondering if he's doing it on purpose.

"What . . . what's going on?" Dad sputters. "What am I supposed to do now?"

The camera cuts to Ray and Symie. "Well, she's dressed for this weather, right, Dan?" she says, referring to the picture.

"Yeah, it really is a hot one, isn't it?" says Ray.

We can still hear Dad stammering in the background.

"And Dan's about to tell us if we can expect a hot Fourth of July. Ah, here we go."

Back to Dad, whose classy silk tie has somehow gotten crooked, whose new glasses have slipped dangerously close to the end of his nose. He pushes them back up, turns to the weather map—the right one at last—and intones, "A hot air mass. Stationary. Looks like sun, sun, sun. For days to come."

He slaps his pointer against the map for emphasis, and it breaks right in half. Dad tumbles backward, sliding down the wall behind him and out of sight.

Quick cut to a commercial.

Nobody says anything for a long minute. Mom just sits there with one hand pressed against her heart, the other over her mouth. Gramps blinks and blinks again. I sit still and feel my heart slide down my body right into my shoes. Poor Dad. Poor, poor Dad. I feel so bad for him. I feel so bad for me.

Finally, Gramps clears his throat. "Well . . . ahem . . . well, it'll get better. *He'll* get better. Before you know it, he'll be an old pro. There's nothing like doing something day in and day out for a few months to whip you into shape."

Mom turns to him slowly. "What are you talking about, a few months?"

Gramps pauses, then announces, "His agent and I got Dan a two-month trial run as the regular TV weatherman."

"Are you kidding?" Mom stares at him in disbelief. "He'll be lucky if he lasts two more days at this job! How *could* you, Pete? How *could* you try to force him into something like that?" she yells.

"How can you keep coddling him, Ellen?" Gramps snaps back. "And I'm not forcing him. He can speak for himself if he doesn't want this job. But he'd be crazy to turn it down. It'll take him places. It'll make him a Big Wheel. Right?" He looked at me.

For a moment I feel like I've been peeking through

the wrong end of a telescope. Then suddenly every-thing's large and clear—only I don't like what I see.

And I blow up. "No. You're not right. You're wrong. You've been wrong the whole time. About everything. Everything!" I shout.

Gramps's jaw drops and Mom's brow wrinkles. They both try to talk at once, but I don't listen. I race out to my bike and pedal away blindly, like a once-upon-a-time high roller whose luck has finally and completely run out.

CHAPTER

SEVENTEEN

The park doesn't help. Neither does the old railroad tracks nor the quarry, where I hoist chunk after chunk of slate and chuck them into the pit. I'm still feeling mad at Gramps, mad at Topper, mad at my gang for getting taken in by Topper, and, most of all, mad, mad, mad at myself. If Gramps is wrong, I'm wronger—for listening to him, for not listening to my gang, for messing up Wild Willie's pool, for hurting Tag's feelings.

Admit it, Wheel. For once in your life, you've blown it but good, I tell myself off as I race through one of the two red lights on Center Street and miss getting hit by a car by inches.

Then, would you believe it, but there's a police car, siren screaming away, chasing me down. I pull over to the curb, and who should get out but, you guessed it, Officers Birdsall and McPhail.

"You're not color blind, are you, Wheel? You can tell the difference between red and green?"

"No, sir. Yes, sir," I say.

"Then how do you explain the fact that you just went through a red light?"

"Stupidity, sir," I reply.

"Not funny," says Birdsall. He doesn't realize I'm not trying to be.

"He's right, Wheel. You or that driver could've been hurt. The same traffic rules for drivers also apply to bike riders," Officer McPhail explains.

I don't have the patience for it. "Okay, then give me a ticket and let me outta here," I tell him.

"Watch that attitude of yours," Birdsall barks.

"Sorry, sir," I mumble. Then, who knows why, but I add, "I'm having a bad day."

Suddenly Birdsall's face softens. He nods at me. "Yeah, we all have those sometimes. Listen, kid, tell your dad to hang in there. My first day on the job was a real stinker, too."

Is there anybody in this town who didn't watch the news at noon? Birdsall's sympathy bugs me even more than his badgering. But I really want out of there bad, so I say, "I'll tell him."

"Good." He lectures me a little more, then finally lets me go.

I pedal away slowly this time, and before I know it, without really planning it, I'm at the Old Wembley Place.

I start to turn around to leave. But then I sigh a

big "I give up" sigh and head to the back of the house, where Topper's sitting by himself on the edge of the pool, watching it drain.

I sit down next to him.

He doesn't look up. Neither of us speaks for a long time. Then he says, "So where'd you get the fish?"

"That was the easy part," I reply.

"Effective," he says, patting his top hat. "Not very subtle. But effective." He sounds like my reading teacher.

"Look," I tell him, "I didn't know your dad was Wild Willie. You could've told me."

"That would have made a difference?"

"Of course it would have. You knew how I felt about Wild Willie."

"But that's not how I wanted to become your friend—by being Wild Willie's kid."

"You didn't want to be my friend. You wanted to steal my gang!" my voice rises.

"Only after you wouldn't let me in it," he raps out.

"Bull! If I'd have let you into my gang, you would've tried to steal it anyway. To take over. You wanted to be the Big Wheel, and you know it. And a gang can't have two Big Wheels," I declare.

Topper turns and looks at me, and I swear, it's weird, but suddenly somehow I feel like I'm looking right at myself. "Why not?" he demands.

"Why not? Why not? Ask the army! Ask the navy! Ask *Star Trek!* There's always just *one* capatin. *One!*"

Topper keeps looking at me. "Well then, who's going to be captain?"

"It sure isn't gonna be you," I toss back.

"What makes you so sure of that?"

"Because I've been the Big Wheel in this town longer than you've been able to tell time. You may think you've got my gang now, but I'll get them back. And when I do, they're gonna stick with me!"

"You've been bullying your gang into sticking with you," Topper jabs.

Bully. Know-it-all. Tyrant. Tag's face and Mike's words and the rest of my gang's voices and my dream flash through my head, and I wince. The kid landed his punch. But quickly, I slug back. "Yeah? Well, you've been *buying* them. With your goodies and your freebies. Your fancy house and your fancy pool. How long do you think it'll be before they figure that out and get tired of you, Mr. Megabucks?"

Blam! That really connects. He chews his lip and blinks. "You think that's the only reason why they like me?" he says like he's trying to scoff at the idea, but the catch in his voice tells me he's afraid that what I've said is true.

It makes me realize he doesn't know—maybe will never know—if people like him for himself or for his money and his dad's fame. And I feel sorry for him. But I don't say a word. I don't get up and leave either. I feel like we're bound together, him and me, and neither of us can—or maybe wants to—break free.

Then who should we see striding across the lawn but Topper's dad (even though I now know he's Wild Willie, I'm still having trouble calling him that).

"Hello, Top. Hi, Wheel. Long time, no see," he salutes, as he heads our way.

Topper can tell from his tone that he's kidding with that last comment, and he gives me a puzzled sideways glance. "My grandfather interviewed your dad for the paper," I tell him. "I went along."

He bobs his head. By now his famous dad has reached us. "What happened here?" he asked, staring down into the almost empty pool.

I shut my eyes, the condemned prisoner at the block.

"Fish," says Topper. "This morning there was a whole mess of stinking fish in the pool."

"There was what?" Wild Willie says in disbelief.

"Cod, I think," Topper offers. "Or maybe haddock."

I bow my head, wishing he'd put me out of my misery and cut it off with one swift, clean stroke.

"Who put it there?" Wild Willie wants to know.

Here it comes at last, I think, steeling myself for the blow.

"Who knows?" is Topper's reply.

"Vandals," says his father, shaking his head. "I thought we'd left them behind in the city."

"More like kids pulling a prank. They probably won't bother us again," Topper assures him.

"How do you know that?"

"Oh, just a hunch." Topper smiles at me.

My breath, which I'd been holding, comes out in a great big whoosh.

Wild Willie looks at me and I'm sure he can see right through me, and Topper, too. But he just shakes his head again and, with real sympathy, says, "Too bad. I invited you to come over for a swim, and this happens."

"Uh . . . buh . . . duh . . . ," I blabber like I'm just learning to talk.

Smooth as pancake syrup, Topper says, "He didn't come for a swim, Dad. He came to ask me to be in the carnival. Right, Wheel?"

Blackmail! The kid, the two-bit sneak thief, is blackmailing me. A squawk starts to make its way out of my mouth, but I squelch it fast. Because the alternative—Wild Willie finding out what I did—is worse. "Right, I'm glad he . . . uh . . . said yes," I answer, trying to sound enthusiastic. Instead I sound like my fingernails are being pulled out one by one.

Topper beams at me. It makes me want to rearrange his face. He turns back to his dad. "I thought that we could have the carnival here at night instead of during the day at Moorland Park. It could be the entertainment for our Fourth of July party, then you could be the emcee after all. We can change the time and the address on the posters around town, ask Wheel's granddad to print the new time and address in the newspaper, get some of the studio guards to handle crowd control, and, bingo, we'll make a lot of money to give to charity."

"What about our privacy, Topper? You want the whole town to know where we live?" asks his dad.

"They're going to know anyway once that article in the *Marietta Messenger* comes out," Topper replies. "You can't keep secrets in a town this size, can you, Wheel?"

"Some of us can," I mutter.

"So come on, Dad. What do you say?" says Topper.

I hold my breath and say a silent prayer.

Wild Willie looks at each of us in turn and scratches his chin. "Hmm," he ponders. "Well . . . why not?"

It takes a moment to sink in. "You mean you're saying yes?" I ask.

"I guess I am," said Wild Willie, with a grin.

"Whoo-wee!" I jump up, pumping the air with my fist. Topper leaps up, too. We're both grinning and high-fiving it while Wild Willie stands there, laughing.

A whiff of fish wafts our way. "Whew!" Wild Willie fans it away. "It's too *fragrant* here for me. See you later." He heads for the house.

Topper and I celebrate a while longer. Then we flop on the grass. He leans on one elbow. "I told you you'd have a better chance of getting Wild Willie for your emcee if you let me be in the show," he lobs, with a smug smile.

"Without me, there wouldn't even *be* a show, Mr. Moneybags!" I smash back.

He just keeps smiling. I'm about to let him have it. And then it hits me. Maybe there won't even *be* a show if I don't get my gang together, and that's going to take some doing.

"Gotta go," I say, scrambling up. "Got a lot to do. Rehearsal here later, okay?"

Topper nods.

I'm halfway across the lawn when I turn. "Oh, yeah. And thanks—you blackmailer!" I call.

Topper grins and tips his hat.

CHAPTER

EIGHTEEN

I call up each and every one of them. "Look, I guess maybe I was a little hard on you," I say. And it isn't easy. But a Big Wheel has to own up to his mistakes.

"Hard? You weren't that bad," says Corey.

"Hard? You made old Dragon Lady Lawrence seem like a pussycat," says Mike, referring to her gym teacher.

"Okay, okay. You don't have to exaggerate. The thing is, it won't happen again. But I need you to come over. Right now. I've got something big— really big—to tell you."

And they show up—Corey and Mike, followed by Tara and Brian, Kwesi and Kong—with their capes and tap shoes, their cards, balls, barbells, and one stuffed gorilla. Only one person is missing. The one I couldn't reach. The one I want to see most of all. Tag.

"So, what's the big news?" asks Tara, not wasting any time.

But I don't want to rush. "I've been having a war council," I say slowly.

Mike catches on immediately. "With Topper?" she says.

"Yes."

"Somebody dumped fish in his pool. Pee-yu, did it stink!" says Tara.

"Yeah, I wonder who did it," says Kwesi, looking right at me.

"I wonder," I reply coolly, staring right back.

"So, what happened at this council?" asks Kong.

"The carnival's off," I say, and pause.

"Off? But we've been rehearsing like crazy," Corey protests. "I've got a whole new juggling act."

"I can stand on my head and burp 'Yankee Doodle Dandy,' " Brian tells me.

"And I can do *ten* magic tricks—good ones," Kwesi brags.

"You can't call off the carnival, Wheel. You can't!" Tara looks ready to cry.

"The carnival's off . . . ," I repeat, ". . . at Moorland Park." Now everyone looks confused. "We're having it instead at . . ." I space out the words dramatically, ". . . the Old Wembley Place, with the one, the only, the Man himself, Wild Willie Smith, hosting the show!"

My gang goes nuts, so nuts with the yelling and cheering, the hugging and high-fiving and telling me I'm the biggest, best thing since Santa Claus, that it's a while before Corey wants to know how it happened and Kwesi asks how come I already know Wild Willie will be emcee when the contest winner hasn't been announced yet.

So then, even though I don't want to, I tell them the rest of the tale, leaving out a few tidbits, such as my being the fishy culprit and Topper's blackmail, and they go even more crazy. "You mean that was Wild Willie all along—Topper's dad?" Brian's eyes bug out.

"Yeah," I have to admit.

"But he wasn't even *funny!*" Tara exclaims.

I burst out laughing, which makes everyone else laugh, too.

Then everybody's quiet a minute, and I wonder if they're thinking about *my* dad and his performance. But nobody says anything, and I don't bring it up.

Instead Tara says, "You've got to see my dance, Wheel. I've added a new time step, three cramp rolls, and wings!" That cracks us up again, until Tara starts to pout, and I stop guffawing.

"Okay, kid, let's see what you've got," I tell her. She turns out to be good, really good, and I let her know it, which makes her light up like a two-hundred-watter.

Everyone wants to show off their act then, and I tell them I can't wait to see them all, but I'm going to—wait, that is. "Big rehearsal tonight. After dinner. At the Old Wemb—at Topper's. See you then," I say.

And I'm off again to do what I've never done before—to apologize to Tag.

He's not home. I wait, get up to leave, sit back down, get up to leave, sit back down. Finally Mrs. McGill's car pulls up, and Tag steps out of it, holding a really big, really stupid-looking doll.

I fight to keep from giggling. You don't giggle in someone's face when you want him to forgive you.

He sees me and comes over, the doll in its box making him waddle. "My cousin Betty's birthday," he tells me, turning red.

"Yeah? I've got a cousin Betty," I respond, like isn't that an amazing coincidence.

Tag smiles a little. Then, realizing he's still mad at me—or he's supposed to be—his mouth goes tight. He frowns at the doll, propping it against a wall.

I pluck a leaf from the azalea bush by the front steps and roll it around in my hand. Mrs. McGill, unloading groceries, waves and walks into the garage. I wave back, even though she's already out of sight, and take a deep breath. I know what I want to say, but suddenly it's hard to say it.

"About yesterday," I begin. "I didn't mean for that to happen to your bike. I'll pay to have it fixed up."

Tag looks surprised but wary. "The bike's already being fixed and you couldn't afford it."

I think about insisting, but he's right—I *couldn't* afford it.

I pull off another leaf and go on. It doesn't get

141

any easier. It's like I suddenly caught a case of shyness flu or something. "I . . . you said some stuff to me . . . tried to warn me I was being a tyrant . . . ," I pause.

"I never said that." Tag shakes his head.

"Well, you wouldn't remember saying it," I tell him, and he looks confused. "But anyway," I continue, "the thing is . . . I guess I was a tyrant, kind of. I pushed you and everyone else around. I didn't listen to what you had to say. I didn't pay attention to . . . to your feelings. And I'm sorry. Really sorry." I can hardly look at him.

Trying to decide whether or not to believe me, he reaches across me and pulls off a couple of azalea leaves. The thing's gonna be naked by the time we finish this conversation.

And I'm the one who has to finish it. "Because . . . because you were right. You're not just some tagalong, Tag. You're my friend. My best friend. And I want to keep it that way."

I know I've said the right thing because, whew, Tag heaves a sigh of relief. "Yeah?" he says.

"Yeah." I punch him in the arm. He punches me back. We sit there for a few moments in friendly silence. Then I ask, "Did you see my dad on TV today?"

"Uh . . . yeah . . . ," I hear him choosing his words carefully. "He . . . uh . . . was . . . unique."

"He was awful. 'Hi, Ray. Hi, Slimy.' " I mimic.

Tag's lips twitch. He tries to hold it in.

" 'Where's the map? Where's the darn map?' " I squawk like a parrot. " 'What am I supposed to do now?' " I wail.

That does it. Tag breaks up, and I join in. Soon we can't stop. " 'We'll have nothing but sun, sun, sun . . . whoops!' " I flop on my back, which makes us laugh harder. It's the second time today I've doubled up, and it feels good. The awful knot I've had in my stomach shakes loose. If Dad were here, I'd hug him. Hard.

"Want to have dinner at my house?" I ask when we finally stop laughing. "Then we'll go over to Topper's for the big rehearsal."

"The what?" Tag's jaw drops.

"Come on. Stop catching flies. Get on your old bike. I'll fill you in on the details on the way," I say. And I do.

I tell him everything, and I mean everything—going back to my executive stress and being stuck for the Fourth of July idea on to pushing everyone too hard and all the way up to yelling at Gramps and my revenge on Topper. Tag's face is a mirror of all the things I've felt. When I get to the bit about discovering whose pool it was I polluted, he's got such a look of horror that I want to console him. So I move on quickly to Topper's scam. He listens closely—nobody can listen the way Tag can—his grin getting wider and wider, especially at the part about Topper blackmailing me.

"That guy is Mr. Slick." He shakes his head in admiration.

"Hey, whose side are you on?" I ask, grinning, too, because I do have to hand it to the kid—he really is Wile E. Coyote in action.

"The side of truth, justice, and the American way!" Tag recites.

"Thank you, Superman," I hail, glad everything's okay between us again.

Then we're at my house. "Uh-oh," says Tag a second before I do. Dad's home. Gramps is still here (or here again). So is Mom. What they're having inside is no tea party, and I don't think I care to join it. But a Big Wheel doesn't run away from a problem.

I expect to hear the shouting before we even get in the door. But instead, there's just one voice— firm, strong, but not loud, coming through the screen.

"I love you, Pop. And I know you love me. But enough's enough. You kept telling me to speak my mind. Well, I'm speaking it now. You can't keep trying to run my life. And I can't keep pretending if I go along with it you'll go away. I don't want to be a TV star—not now, not ever!"

Tag and I look at each other, tiptoe toward the kitchen, and peek in.

Dad is standing in front of Gramps, letting him have it. Gramps is sitting there, taking it. Behind them both, Mom is shadowboxing. When she sees me and Tag, she stops right/lefting it and gives us a big thumbs-up.

I hesitate, trying to figure out how I feel. I look

144

at Dad again. He seems taller all of a sudden. And Gramps, yeah, he's shocked. But at the same time, would you believe it, he looks tickled to death. I switch back to Mom, who's grinning. I return her thumbs-up. Then Tag and I slip quietly out of the house.

"Uh, my mom's making franks and beans for dinner," says my best friend, after a moment or two.

"Sounds good to me," I say as we get on our bikes. "Real, real good."

C H A P T E R

N I N E T E E N

oh. Ahh," goes the audience as Mike, with the spotlight on her, slowly stands up with a barbell in her hands and Corey, curling a set of weights, on her shoulders. "Yes!" she declares. She's got the audience where she wants them, and she's loving every minute of it.

Onstage everything is perfect. Backstage, which is a big tent Wild Willie has had set up for us, everything is not. Brian can't fix his bow tie. Kwesi can't find his magic silks. Kong has skinned his elbow. Tag is green with stage fright. Tara's costume is ripped.

Where's my mother when I need her? Sitting in the audience, oohing and ahhing with the rest of the mothers and fathers. Where am I? Standing there with a needle and thread, sewing Tara's shoulder strap.

"Don't stick me. Don't stick me," she whines.

"I won't if you stop wiggling," I say. Who needs my mother, I think. I've turned into her.

"I'm a great biker. I'm a great biker," Tag, following my advice, is repeating over and over. It doesn't seem to be working.

Then Topper comes over. "I already told you," I say before he can get out a word. "You're next to last. Last is the grand finale, and the grand finale is me and Tag."

"Fine," he says.

"Fine?" I give him a suspicious look. "Did you say fine?"

"That's right." He smiles innocently at me, which makes me even more suspicious. "I just came to see if you need any help."

I'm about to tell him thanks but no thanks, everything's under control, but the fact is I've decided that it's okay for a Big Wheel to accept a helping hand when needed—even if it's from a blackmailing sneak thief named Topper Smith. So I say, "Yeah. You got a pair of sunglasses I can borrow?" I don't tell him I left mine at home. And he doesn't ask.

"Sure. In the house. I'll get them for you."

"Thanks," I say.

"I *am* a great biker. I *am* a great biker," Tag's voice rises.

"That's right, you are," I encourage him. "And soon everyone else will know it, too."

"Urp," he says and bolts out of the tent.

"Maybe I should get a bucket, too." Topper

smirks. Sometimes I still want to smack the guy.

He leaves, and Mike and Corey come backstage, arguing. "You almost dropped me," he complains.

"You were kicking my back!" she yells.

They both look at me.

"It was great!" I say.

"Yeah. Wasn't it?" They both grin and go right back to arguing.

Onstage Wild Willie is doing his emcee number. He's just as good live as he is on the radio. "Man," he says, "that last act made me want to take my vitamins, eat my spinach, wolf down some Wheaties, liquefy some liver—and then take a good, long nap. I used to be an exercise freak, but no more. Other animals don't work out, so why should I? Elephants are the strongest mammals on earth, and do they go jogging? No, Joe. Tortoises, they live the longest, and you don't see them puffing away on the old Stairmaster. Right, Dwight? And gorillas, the day I see one using a rowing machine, I'll go swing in the jungle, Jim. . . . By the way, where does a five-hundred-pound gorilla sit?"

"Anywhere he likes," half of the audience answers.

"What did the lovesick gorilla say to the chimp?" Wild Willie throws out.

"I go ape over you," this time everybody replies.

"Why did King Kong climb the Empire State Building instead of the Eiffel Tower?"

Just one person responds. It's my mother. "The

148

fare was cheaper to New York," she says, and everyone cracks up, Wild Willie included.

"Speaking of gorillas," he says, "get ready to meet the roughest, toughest ape you'll ever see— the one, the only, King! And in the ring with him, Kong, the fiercest gorilla wrestler in the world!"

Kong bounds out onstage in a fake leopard-skin outfit. He shows off a while, posing and stuff. Then he opens a crate. King's sitting there. Kong taunts him, then pulls him out and finally starts wrestling. He really gets into it, throwing himself and the stuffed ape all over the place, while the audience roars and roars.

They roar at Brian, too, burping his best. They ooh and ahh again at Kwesi, even when he blows the egg trick as usual. They aww, Isn't she cute, at Tara. By the time Topper hands me the sunglasses I asked him to get and steps onstage, they're ready for anything.

And what they get is *something*. From the moment Topper goes hopping up the steps to the stage on his unicycle, juggling three fake cactuses, the audience is his. Every jump, turn, spin, toss, and catch is greeted with applause and cheers that get louder and louder until his dad pitches three fat sticks at him. Still on his unicycle, the kid pulls a lighter out of his pocket, and the sticks become torches. Then a hush falls over the crowd. Tense, they lean forward in their seats as Topper begins to juggle those torches, changing directions and patterns, hypnotizing everyone who's watching. Then one, two, three, he catches them together in one hand, and blows them out. The audience goes berserk, yelling and stomping and demanding an encore, which Topper's only too happy to perform—with four radios and a mini-TV!

No wonder the kid stopped putting up a fuss about going next to last. Who can follow an act like that? I turn to Tag. He doesn't look so green anymore—he looks like he's been hit over the head with a brick.

Topper finishes taking his bows and rides offstage into the tent. "Guess they liked it," he says offhandedly, and goes over to the jug to get some lemonade.

I can think of plenty to say, but none of it is going to help me and Tag up there onstage, or even help me *get* Tag up there onstage.

While our crew is setting up our course and Wild Willie is working the crowd and I'm trying to figure out what to do, Gramps appears.

Things are okay between us again—sort of. I mean I'm not mad at him, and I've apologized for yelling and all that. But I guess I don't have so much faith in his tips anymore.

"Great show so far," he says.

"Thanks." I try to sound enthusiastic, but it comes out glum.

That's not what Gramps wants to hear. "What's this?" he demands. "Big Wheels don't sulk."

"We're supposed to be the grand finale," I say

reluctantly because I don't want to admit how dis-couraged I am and get a whole bunch of advice.

"So?"

"So, it looked to me like Topper already stopped the show."

"So what? A show can be stopped more than once," Gramps says and launches into some story about a star who was ready to sing her big number in a show. But the guy who went on before her had a big number, too, singing the names of a zillion Russian composers in something like thirty-nine seconds, and he stopped the show cold.

"What did she do?" asks Gramps. "She did what any great star does—she topped the showstopper. Remember, Wheel, cream always rises to the top. You want to be a star, stop thinking like low-fat yogurt."

I nod, knowing I'm supposed to believe him, but this time I can't.

Besides, Tag's frozen in place, and I figure the last thing *he* wants to believe right now is Gramps's advice. I pull him aside. His eyes are glazed over. "Forget Gramps. You're right—sometimes he's wrong. Dead wrong," I say.

Tag's eyes close. I glance out onstage. The crew's almost finished. Wild Willie's getting set to intro-duce us, and a ball of cold, hard panic is sitting in my gut. "Come on, Tag. Don't let me down now. If we're not brilliant, it's okay as long as we—"

Tag's eyes snap open so suddenly, I jump. "Sometimes your gramps *is* right," he rallies. "Like now. We can do it, Wheel. We can top Topper!"

"You're sure?" I ask.

"You bet!" he exclaims.

That's all I need. The old heart starts pumping harder. The old muscles start flexing and unwinding. Yes, kid, there can be two captains. And yes again, two—no, three—stars.

I turn to Gramps. He's smiling at me from across the floor. "A Big Wheel has to figure out when an old bigmouth's tips are pure hogwash—or pure gold," he broadcasts. I let out a laugh. He opens his arms, and I run into them. He hugs me, and I hug him back.

Then I whirl around and slip on those Daredevil Biker shades. "Come on, Tag!" I bellow. "Let's bring down the house!"

And, of course, we do. By the time we fly, perfectly synchronized, over the stacked hibachis and the kiddie pool and land, bip, precisely on the white finish line taped to the stage, the audience is stamping and shouting so loud they've gotta be hearing them over in the next state.

Before all of those cheering people, Tag and I, holding up each other's hands like prizefighters, take our bows. And it feels great. I see my mom in the front row whoo-whooing it and Dad—Dad!— with his fingers in his mouth, making like a train whistle. Next to them, Gramps is, what else, taking notes, and the *Marietta Messenger* photographer is taking a picture. And there are Tag's folks and the rest of my gang's; Ms. Ridley and Mr. LoVecchio, would you believe, smooching; Officer Birdsdall with his wife and six kids; and Officer McPhail with his Great Dane.

"Look, Tag," I say, "there's Gina Suzuki."

He turns red and almost falls off the stage.

There are lots of other people I know, and some I don't, and all of them are glowing in the flood-lights playing over the audience and the stage.

I turn my head and see Topper, off to one side, and he should be annoyed, I think, because we did it—we topped him! But he's shaking his head and grinning like that old canary-chomping cat. I bet he's taking credit for Tag's and my performance, like he made us be that good, and, guess what, I don't even care. I motion for him to come onstage, and the crowd goes wild. Then I call out the rest of my gang, and finally Wild Willie, and suddenly we're all bowing to and applauding each other, and it feels more than great. It feels just right.

Then there's a big *kaboom*, and we all look up to see a golden rocket shower down a thousand little stars, followed by another starburst and another.

I slap Topper and Tag on the back. They do the same to me. As we ooh and we ahh at those corny and beautiful fireworks lighting up the sky, I think if this were a movie I was directing, right about now is when I'd flash "The End" in big red, white, and blue letters across the wide, wide screen.